H A

BOOK 1
OF MASKS AND CHROMES

Roberto Ricci

www.theredharlequin.com
Facebook.com/TheRedHarlequin

Cover Illustrations by Pascal Demure
www.pascaldemure.fr

ISBN-10: 1477566899

ISBN-13: 978-1477566893

The Red Harlequin

BOOK 1

Of Masks And Chromes

Roberto Ricci

Table of Contents

◆

No one really knows how Harlequins came to be.
The Collective Laws do not mention them.
Nor are they described in the sacred books.
And yet they exist.
Some say they were the result of cross breeding
between different colors of chromes. Others say they
were sent by the gods to remind us how fortunate we
chromes really are.
All I know is that Harlequins can simulate any of our
colors.
They can talk like us; act like us and sometimes even
fight like us.
But they are not like us.
When an animal has been slaughtered, or an infant is
found dead, a Harlequin is surely among us.
That is why he must be found quickly.
And put immediately to death.

1. Death of a Harlequin

I had almost reached my fourteenth solstice when my father decided the time had come for me to witness my first execution. The execution of a Harlequin.

"You must learn how to recognize a Harlequin when you see one," he said.

The thought of seeing a real live Harlequin in the flesh frightened and excited me so much that when he came to wake me that cold and sunless morning, I was already dressed and ready. I had barely slept at all.

A few moments later, with our cloaks wrapped around us and fortified by hot herbal broth to ward off the cold, we paused by the front door to put our masks on. As we did, my father cast me a glance up and down and smiled.

"I'm sure you get taller with every sunrise, Asheva."

"And more like you," said my mother.

She had slipped quietly out from her bedroom.

I sensed it was important to her that she see me before I left; like she knew my eyes were about to be opened to the brutal reality of the world and she wanted to prepare me for it in whatever small way she could, even if that meant placing my mask over my face herself, fixing it straight and brushing my hair back over it.

"That's a good thing, isn't it?" said my father with a wry smile at her.

"Yes," she said, her eyes fixed on my blood-red, crimson mask of death with its black lips and tears, made for me by her own mother. "It is." There was trepidation and unease in her voice which my father ignored; he may not have liked the idea of what lay ahead of us any more than she did, but he knew that it had to be done.

He put his own simple black and white mask on, glancing in to the mirror to adjust it. There was might and strength in every part of him, from his height, to the power of his shoulders, the broadness of his back and even the thickness of his hands and fingers which settled his mask in place with delicate dexterity. He was our guide and protector; strong, fair, brave and indestructible. He was a hero, a veteran of wars against both the Blue Chromes and the Red. It is hard to describe the intense swell of pride that being his son gave me. From as early as I could remember, the only thing I wanted in life was to be like him. With a final hug each for my mother, we stepped out in to the chilly, gloomy dawn.

Side by side, my father and I wound our way down the steep, cobbled streets of Axyum, our great and ancient city. Though it was early, the streets were crowded with our fellow Black Chromes. With our long, wool cloaks brushing the ground around our legs as we went, we must have looked like a procession of ungainly, flightless crows. Every step intensified the burning sense of unease in my stomach; the tug of war between terror and excitement. By the time we joined the large crowd gathered in Victory Square, under the watchful glare of statues and monuments to fallen heroes of past Chrome wars, a chill wind had had begun to whip in from the east and I could feel the first light drops of rain starting to fall.

At the center of the square stood the gallows pole. Sturdy, splintered and blood-stained; it was a forbidding portent of what was to come. Around the edges of the square were tribune stands; pulpitums which had been erected for dignitaries to watch the execution from in prominence. They were all filled with black chromes apart from one on which a clutch of figures dressed variously in shades of white, violet, yellow and blue stood; it was impossible for your gaze not to be drawn towards them.

I turned to my father.

"Why are they here?"

"Dignitaries from other Territories are always invited to witness the execution of a Harlequin," he replied. "They are as much their enemies as ours."

There were four of them. One was in a white mantle but his mask and belt marked him out as the emissary of the Violets; there were two dressed in blue velvet while the fourth, in a rich saffron cloak of calfskin with a golden mask represented the Yellows. I sensed an unease about them, confined in their small stand, surrounded by a sea of somber, simple Blacks.

"Where are the Orange and the Red?" I asked my father.

He took a moment to look carefully at them all before replying.

"I don't know."

He was disturbed. Clearly for him, the absence of two other colors was significant and not a good sign; especially in the case of the Reds, our greatest enemies and against whom we had fought so many wars over the centuries. I was about to ask him to tell me more. But as I did, a great roar went up, starting from the opposite side of the square and then spreading over towards us. The execution procession had arrived.

I could see two black flags bob and weave their way towards the gallows pole. Everyone around us pressed in close and strained for the best view. I felt a slight panic rise in my chest at the prospect of what I was about to witness and as bodies moved ever more tightly together and began to pin me in. As tight, guttural cries of anger rose around me and all eyes were directed towards the flags, I was pretty certain no one would notice if I was crushed or even dragged under their feet. I reached out for my father's arm to steady myself. He saw the fear in my eyes.

"Be calm," he shouted, above the rising din. "No matter what happens. Understand?"

I nodded and did my best to show him I wasn't scared. Nothing frightened me more than the idea of disappointing him.

The flags were accompanied by the tattoo of drums. Their rhythmic cadence was so powerful they vibrated deep in my chest like an invading heartbeat. Within moments, the loud murmur and commotion of voices died away and a hush fell across the crowd. When the drums stopped a moment or so after that, the silence that engulfed the square was so profound and intense it was as if the gods themselves had cast a muted spell upon the city.

I can't remember how long it lasted for. It felt like hours, but might only have been as long as three or four beats of the heart. What I will never forget is the way it was shattered by a piercing shriek of terror as a figure appeared above the crowd.

There was the Harlequin.

He was borne on a wooden platform, carried on the shoulders of several guards. Strapped to a ladder, his hands were bound behind his back. As he jerked and lurched across the square towards us, I could see a swine's head had been placed on top of his own, its skin stretched tight around his skull and down over his forehead. The pig's blood trickled and flowed down the Harlequin's face to mingle with his own which oozed from cuts all around his eyes and gashes in his cheeks where he had been beaten. He was dressed in robes of many colors, the like I had never before seen. Garish, sickly patches of red, yellow, green and blue had been stitched together in jarring, disturbing patterns. It was an abominable sight.

The Harlequin cried out again; a lamenting wail of fear. This time it was answered by a full-blown roar of rage and vitriol from the crowd; starting amongst a small number near where he passed and then spreading out as a feverish hatred gripped the square. I turned to my father again.

"Could he be the Red Harlequin?" I whispered in his ear.

There was no more reviled and feared figure in all of the territories. Said to be the leader and master of all Harlequins, the very mention of him struck terror in to us when we were young. Legends and stories about him abounded, many of them made up to scare us, but they stuck in the mind nonetheless; for a long time, I truly believed that he had turned red after drinking the blood of children. Whether or not that was true, one thing was beyond certain. He was real.

My father didn't reply. Like everyone else around us, his eyes were on the prisoner. I looked once more at the blood-soaked, grotesque figure. Though he was bound and secured, how could I be sure that he didn't have the power to break free and kill us all?

"What if he flies away?" I asked.

"He won't. He's been strapped well. Be strong, Asheva."

I nodded and looked back at the Harlequin. He was getting ever closer and in a moment or so I would be able to see him more clearly. What I expected, I wasn't sure. But as he neared the gallows, I was surprised to see a creature that looked no different than me and was only a few solstices older, barely twenty as far as I could guess. I remember being struck by his exposed face. Chromes wear masks in public, regardless of their color; it is one of the Collective Laws. So the sharp contrast of crimson blood on his pale white face was perhaps the most shocking thing of all. To be gazed upon by so many eyes in such a state was an almost unfathomable humiliation. I felt intense embarrassment for him.

He tilted his petrified eyes upwards, no doubt making one final, desperate plea to the gods to rescue him.

As he did, the pig's head fell off. The crowd laughed and jeered. I tried to join in, feeling it was my duty. But I couldn't. I was unable to harden my heart towards him. Pity welled inside me.

"How do you know he is a Harlequin?" I asked my father.

"You'll see in a moment," he said.

There was something in his voice which made me realize that he was as uneasy as I was about bearing witness to what was about to happen. Nonetheless, as he now raised his voice against the creature along with the rest of the crowd, it was filled with convincing enough disdain.

The Harlequin began to shake violently. And as he did, I found it hard to imagine him as dangerous or clever. What sort of mischief could he have committed to deserve such an end? It took two guards to keep him still as a third looped the noose around his neck.

They were set to push him from the ladder, when he cried out, his voice cutting through the insults and the venomous jeers.

"Please! I beg of you for mercy. I am not a Harlequin!"

And as he said it, I swear on all of the gods, he looked straight at me.

His words echoed about the square for a moment or more before the guards wrested the ladder away from him and his body swung out over our heads in a wide arc. It jerked violently for what seemed like an eternity. I couldn't look. I turned my head away, but my father reached out and clasping a large hand around the back of my skull turned it back again.

"Watch," he said.

A mist of rainbow colors had formed beneath the swinging, twitching feet of the dead Harlequin. They swirled outwards and hung in the air for a few short moments, long enough for astonished gasps and murmurs to rise across the crowd. And then, as quickly as they had appeared, they vanished. A great cheer went up.

"What was that? "I asked, though I suspected I knew the answer.

Another Chrome to my right answered before my father could, his eyes wild with hatred and repugnance. "That was the filthy, evil creature's aura, leaving its body!" he said. "And good riddance!" He bellowed again, so loudly it stung my ear, "good riddance!"

I searched for any sense of relief or rejoicing inside myself at the 'creature's death, but I couldn't find any. All I could see, seared in to my mind, were his eyes staring at me in the seconds before his death, like a cornered forest deer set to be slaughtered at the end of a hunt.

The clouds broke above us and the rain began to fall in earnest. The crowd began to quickly disperse, few being bothered to stay and watch the body be cut down by the guards and tossed on to a cart to be wheeled away and later burnt. The show was over. There was now the humdrum business of the day to attend to. Chromes headed off in every direction, like a receding black tide, along alleys and roads leading away from Victory Square. Some made their way to the nearest taverns, eager to toast to hearts that still beat.

My father and I returned home to my mother. She didn't ask me how I felt. She didn't have to. One look at me and she could tell very well.

For the rest of that day and for several after, I focused on how glad I was to still be alive. I breathed deep the air, I ate well and appreciated every mouthful. I took care to soak up every detail around me, to live as if every hour might be my last. As I would fall in to my bed each night, I would thank the gods that I was not a Harlequin and pray fiercely that I might never encounter another one as long as I lived. Since that time, I have often wondered if those prayers were too much temptation for the gods.

Safe to say they went unanswered.

2. The Black Nation

The next morning, I was awoken by the sound of proclamations in the streets. Messengers had been sent out across the city to instruct every citizen to gather in front of the Palace of the Elders by midmorning. The Eldest himself was going to address us.

"Hurry! Put on your robes," said my mother.

Though I didn't want to admit it, I was still shaken by the events of the day before. The idea of gathering in a crowd once more did not appeal to me.

"Must we go?" I asked her.

"Just do as your mother tells you," snapped my father, irritably. He almost never raised his voice. Looking back, I wonder if he already knew then what this gathering was going to mean for our family.

"Here, wear this," my mother said, in a more soothing tone, casting father a small, reproachful glance. She handed me my black mask. A gift from my father, delicately carved from a thin sheet of onyx, to me it was more precious than gold and I only wore it on the most important occasions. Our black masks were to be used only for proclamation of a festivity, the death of an elder, or war. The next festivity was still far away in the calendar and no news of an elder's death had reached our house. That left only one possibility. And if I had any doubts about it, the look in my father's eyes put them to rest.

By the time the three of us arrived at the palace, most of the city had already gathered. As we squeezed our way through the crowds, the tension was palpable and no one dared speak, not even to whisper to the chrome next to them. The Elders stood on the palace's marble stairs. Unlike our sturdy wool black cloaks, their robes were made of finely spun silk and their black masks were finely decorated with gold ornaments. But even among such splendor, there was one mask that shined brightest; the mask of The Eldest – the most beautiful I had ever seen. Fashioned of black gold, Andahar had told me it was older than time, having been made by Lapis, the shepherd god and protector of our nation, as a gift to the very first Black eldest.

Standing before us, with the elders lined solemnly behind him, the Eldest's deep voice boomed out, commanding our attention. He measured his words carefully to make sure everyone understood the gravity of the situation.

"Devout sons and daughters of the Black nation, the gods are listening!" he began, spreading his arms wide. "This morning, a herald of the Red chromes delivered to us a vile, treacherous message. A message we have been long expecting. They have declared war against us! Against the gods' chosen, the most honorable and ancient nation of the chromes!"

The response was immediate. Cries of outrage, anger and dismay went up all around us. It took the guards several moments to hush us so that the Eldest could continue.

"My brothers and sisters, they want to invade the land given to us by our ancestors!' he cried, his voice cracking with indignant fury. 'They have already occupied part of the Eastern forest."

As the Eldest spoke, I felt a profound admiration for him. I had never seen his face, but like all of us Black chromes, my devotion to him was total and unquestioning. I knew that there was not a single chrome gathered around me who doubted that his wisdom, courage and strength would lead us to victory. His solemn voice echoed throughout the city. "The First Army will quickly be mustered. They will prepare to move in the direction of the Eastern forest."

The First Army consisted of our most experienced warriors, the primary line of defense in case of an attack. It also bought precious preparation time for the Second and Third Armies, made up of younger and lesser trained chromes. Having fought valiantly in two of the toughest wars our nation had ever endured, my father was a battle-scarred veteran of the First Army, a real warrior who had experienced first-hand the atrocities of combat; the loss of friends and the fear of death. He never spoke of it to me, other than to tell me that "in war there are no chrome winners. The only victor is Jaries, the god of war and vengeance, who yearns for blood to spill from every chrome, regardless of color. In the end, his thirst is always quenched."

As I lay in bed that night, I heard my mother crying and my father gently consoling her. Despite my father's cautioning words about the reality of war, I felt only excitement and intense pride. I knew that he would defeat the Reds. He was so strong and clever, he seemed invincible. I thought only of the glory he would bring to our house and family name. None of my friends at the seminary had fathers in the First Army! I was certain to be envied. Looking back, I am haunted by my naive certainty. I was young but was I also stupid and selfish?

The days that followed were all about preparation for war. The streets bustled with chromes shouting and running about, with carriages full of armor, food, water and weapons making their way from one end of the city to the other. To demonstrate the supremacy of the Black nation over our enemy we added a torn red flag below our nation's black flag on the mast in front of the Palace of the Elders.

By the third evening after the proclamation, the preparations were complete. The Eastern gates swung open for the First Army to march out to glorious victory. My father had once told me that they marched in the night and fought during the day. As the sun disappeared behind the mountains, a thousand torches lit up the streets of Axyum to guide our soldiers on their way. My mother and I watched from a gate tower while our assembled Legionaries bowed their masked faces en masse for the Eldest's final blessing.

The 'Ceremony of Departure' begged favors from all the gods, but mostly it sought the protection of Jaries, the God of War. An altar had been placed at the entrance of the city. The Eldest raised his arms high and shouted: "Supreme God, father to all the other gods, sacred shepherd of the Black nation, accept this offer to your courage, to your greatness, to your audacity! Bless our warriors with your strength and your guidance! Bring them victory!"

Two guards led a lamb up to the altar. The Eldest raised a knife so that everyone – below the walls and above in the towers – could see it.

"Mighty Jaries, the Black nation calls you," he said. "Let our swords be guided by your wrath. Let the Reds' blood be the wine of your feasts. Fight with us! Fight for us!" Then, covering his dagger with a red cloth as the name of Jaries rang throughout the valley, he stabbed the lamb without mercy until it died.

Now the moment had finally come for the soldiers to depart. I could not recognize my father amongst so many valiant warriors, yet I knew that he was there, the best amongst the best, with his golden armor, his bronze war mask and his black mantle fluttering in the wind.

I had watched him earlier that day as he methodically prepared his armor and his swords. His movements were slow and precise as he sharpened and greased his blade. When he realized I was watching he beckoned me over. I was afraid he was going to scold me. Instead, he placed his large hand over my face and I could smell the oily grease on him. He gently kissed my hair and then went back to his arms. Finally, before leaving our house to join his brothers in arms, he had looked at me one last time and said, "The gods will be telling me whether you've been good or not while I'm away," He smiled but his voice betrayed the heaviness of his heart.

And now the Black warriors were marching out of the gate. They resembled divine furies ready to punish the Red army and restore Black supremacy over all the chromes. I cheered and waved, hoping my father would see me. I studied my friends, watching the spectacle from my same tower and, at that moment, I felt sorry for them. They would never know what a privilege it was to see their fathers go to war to defend the honor of our nation.

Sure enough, as we walked home after the last carriage that night my friend Andahar said "You are lucky to have a father like him. My father has to stay here."

"Why?" I asked.

"Because he is needed by the elders." Then, changing subject, he asked: "How are you preparing for the Rite?"

The Rite of Initiation brought a Black chrome from youth into adulthood. Upon the fourteenth solstice of their birth year, seminarians journeyed into the sacred forests with a group of elders. Deep in the woods, for two weeks, they were taught the story of our nation, after which the elders revealed the 'Collective Laws'. There were also physical trials, including forest hunts and athletic competitions. Only upon their return, were the initiated solemnly proclaimed sons and daughters of the Black nation.

Then, and only then, could they pledge their loyalty and their lives to Axyum.

The build up to the Rite was very intense. Anyone of my age constantly speculated about what could happen to us outside the safety and comfort of our walls. We especially fretted over a horrific rumor that revolved around one seminarian who had lost his life trying to kill a wolf, a story gleefully handed down to us by older brothers or sisters who had succeeded in the Rite and so felt free to tease. They were very tight-lipped about the facts.

"I run along the walls of the city," I told him. "It's dangerous. There are sharp inclines and broken cobblestones. If you fall, you die." Andahar looked at me, not sure if I was joking with him or not. "We can race it together if you want," I said. "Unless you're scared?"

"Of course I'm not," said Andahar, not sounding very convinced.

"Come on then!" I said, and took off.

Andahar sprinted after me. "Hey, that's not fair!" I heard him shout behind me. We ran together along the wall, clinging to the inclines, going tight around turns with steep drops falling away to the side, leaping over gaps and swerving around smashed cobbles, laughing hard all the way until both of us stopped exhausted, near the Western gates to catch finally our breath. Andahar looked at me. "When our time will come to go to battle I want you beside me," he said, surprising me.

"Don't worry," I replied, smiling. "Someone will have to be there to look after you."

We headed home, parting at the top of our alley with Andahar promising that he would beat me next time. I entered my house, where I was hit by a sudden and overwhelming sadness. I watched as my mother, already back before me, tried to keep herself busy by making a hearth fire. After a while her eyes met mine for a moment, but that was all it took. We both started crying, for we knew we could never fill the cold emptiness no matter how much we fed that fire.

Days came and went. I eagerly awaited news from the front. My mornings at the seminary seemed to last an eternity. It was only at dusk that I came alive again. Andahar and I would go with our friends to the palace steps to listen to the Orator's reports from the war front. The Orator was the only chrome besides the elders authorized to speak about the war in public – to avoid any false messages being sent by the enemy to discourage us - we hung on his every word.

The Orator stood at a pulpit in front of the Palace of the Elders. He wore a scarlet-colored mask with a mouth hole shaped like a trumpet which amplified his words so that they resonated throughout the square, penetrating through the walls of Axyum and into the souls of its inhabitants. His mantle was black outside and white inside so that everyone could recognize him. Behind him, three warriors enacted his words in a mime, bringing them vividly to life for all those gathered.

"Brothers and Sisters of the Black Nation!" he began, "I bring you stories of heroism!"

The warriors behind him spread their arms wide and the crowd huzzahed.

"Tales of audacity!" Another cheer as the three tilted their heads skywards.

"And tales of sacrifice!"

This time, the crowd remained silent. The warriors bowed their heads and placed their hands on their hearts.

"Tonight I shall tell you the story of the valiant Legion of the Hawks!"

"That's my father's legion!" I shouted to my friends.

"As you all know, the Reds, in an act of cowardice, invaded our sacred forests before announcing the war."

We all booed.

"Our brave Hawk legionaries, disguised as trees, made their way inside the forest. Aided by Noxa, the goddess of darkness, they moved silently amongst spruces and firs. They remained so still, no one could determine which was tree and which was chrome."

He paused for added dramatic effect, knowing that he had us in the palm of his hand, agog with anticipation. The three figures behind him struck poses describing the legionaries' stealthy progress through the forest.

"Noxa then cast a spell on the forest, making the entire Red army fall asleep. It was then that the trees... came alive!" The Orator unsheathed his sword. "The Reds were not granted enough time to wake and fight death's joyful embrace." As the warriors behind him fended off blow after imaginary blow, his voice became ever louder and more proclamatory. "One by one, our legionaries slew each of them. Red chrome blood flowed through the forest like a river. Oh yes! Hear me! When dawn arrived, the only 'red' that remained in the forest was their blood spilled on the real trees! The Sacred forest was once again Black!"

As the messenger raised his sword and the three warriors their fists to acclaim victory, everyone cheered and clapped for another battle won by our nation. Andahar and I went over these stories time and time again with our friends, embellishing details and creating a few of our own. I imagined my father wading through hordes of Red soldiers at the head of the Hawks, cutting them down and scattering them like chaff in the wind.

It never occurred to me that the messenger did not speak of death or defeat. Those things, I learned, were only to be discussed privately, behind closed doors.

Meanwhile, my life continued much as it had before. Every day I went to the seminary to study for the Rite of Initiation, although I was constantly distracting by thinking about my father and the war.

One day, after we all gathered at the seminary in front of our Headmaster, he scolded us, declaring we were the most unprepared group he'd ever laid eyes on. "When the time comes for the Rite, you must be ready to perform it without fear. The gods have chosen us, the Black nation over all the other chromes for this ritual because they know we are not afraid to suffer. Only those of you who accept pain and have the courage to work your way through it will be successful."

Our Headmaster's name was Paetco and he was

one of the few adults we regularly saw without a mask, for inside seminary walls, none was needed. He was a tall, skinny chrome with a frowning brow and bulging eyes that made him look demonic. None of us ever dared to challenge him – except for Andahar. He had the great misfortune to mock Paetco once, not knowing the Headmaster stood behind him, brandishing a rod. Paetco had my friend whipped in front of the entire seminary, after making sure Andahar's embarrassed mother and father showed up to watch.

"Are you with us, Asheva?" The Headmaster's voice now intruded upon my thoughts.

I felt my face grow warm. "I was thinking about my Father," I stammered. "I am sorry, Master. But I often wonder –"

"How he fares? If he is safe?" The Master limped toward me. Rumor had it that he was a wounded veteran, so I guess I expected him to be sympathetic. "When he comes home – and I have no doubt he will come home, surely you'll wish to greet him as one warrior would another? How proud your father will be to find his son so changed. That is of course, *if* you pass the Rite."

I hung my head and he put his hand on my shoulder. "You can neither know nor control what is going on in the Eastern forest, Asheva. But you can control your life, here. Obey the gods, the elders and myself – that is the greatest thing you could ever do for your father. A warrior like him takes pride in his duty to Axyum and in our traditions, yes?"

I nodded.

"Then let us waste no more time. Everyone come with me."

We followed him into our seminary courtyard. Before hiding our boyish faces behind our masks, I happened to glance sideways at Andahar, who wore a puzzled look on his face identical my own. What new torment could the Headmaster have in store for us?

Outside, from beyond the walls, we heard the voices of our female counterparts. They were chanting an ode to Lyucydia, goddess of wit. I secretly hoped she would favor us with some, for a small part of me couldn't help but wonder if the Rite was a waste of time. Why would the gods, who were so benevolent with our nation, wish us to suffer so? I immediately felt guilty for having such blasphemous thoughts.

The Headmaster stopped in front of a mound of earth, surrounding a large hole. His mask was a grim black affair, with sharp mother-of-pearl ornaments mounted above his eyes. It always made him look so displeased. "Now then," he addressed us. "I am sure that outside these walls you chatter about the Rite, fretting like infants about what is in store for you." He paused for a moment, relishing our unease. "Today, I am pleased to offer you a little taste of your future. Asheva, step forward."

My stomach lurched as I did, desperate to hide my trepidation and fear from the others.

"Bare your arm," he said. I rolled up the sleeve from my left arm. "Kneel and put your entire arm inside this hole." Trying to stop from shaking, I did as I was told. "All the way down" he said. I pushed my arm in as far as it would go. As I did, I began to feel something tickle. Suddenly, the tickle turned to pain, as if a thousand thorns had penetrated my skin, gouging their way inside me.

I cried out and quickly removed my arm. It was full of bloody, crawling dots. Everyone backed away from me. "Borio ants," the Headmaster grinned, while I frantically brushed them off. "These creatures are tiny, yet dangerous." That same tone of pleasure he'd expressed during Andahar's whipping now tinged his voice as he spoke to me. I forced myself to hold my temper. "Thankfully, their bites are not lethal. Asheva didn't know what he was getting into, but now all of you have the advantage... or disadvantage, of witnessing his experience. I want you all to develop a taste for this pain. Because, mark my words, during the Rite –you will long for the good old days you spent with my Borios!"

Later that day, as we chanted and sang odes to the gods, like our female counterparts, the chants and songs served as an outlet for the excruciating agony of the ant bites. We screamed our way through the passages, each one of us determined not to cry in front of the others. Once the sun began to set, we were all grateful that our long day at the seminary had drawn to a close. Before leaving, we thanked the Headmaster for his instruction, as was customary. When it was my turn, I bowed low.

"It was my privilege to serve you, Master," I said.

His eyes glittered with satisfied arrogance. "Asheva, when I told you to put your hand inside that hole, you followed my command without asking what was down there. I am pleased by your unquestioning obedience and loyalty."

Andahar and I left the seminary in silence, dragging our feet. The burning sensation of the venom inside our arms was still very strong. "Do you think the venom will go away?" I said.

"It has to," he replied. "Otherwise, all the adults would still be walking with a limp arm from their seminary days."

I nodded. Then, suppressing a chuckle inside my mask, I imitated Headmaster Paetco: "Andahar, when I told you to place your insolent face in the manure, you followed my command without asking why. I am pleased by your unquestioning obedience and loyalty."

Andahar turned towards me and replied with the same solemnity: "No, it is I that am pleased by your show of loyalty, Asheva. When I told you to place your nose behind the horse's arse and wait for his response not only did you obey, you also seemed quite to enjoy it."

Despite the pain, we laughed all the way home.

3. The Eldest

Forty days after the proclamation of war, a silver-masked messenger knocked at our door. His slim, boney hands fluttered like moths against the black cloth of his robe. "You have been summoned to the palace," he told my mother. "At once. You are also to bring your son." Then, without waiting for a response, he left.

"Surely it is to further prepare you for the Rite," said my mother as we hurried to the main square. "Or perhaps the Forests are no longer safe and they wish to hold it somewhere else."

The thought that I would not make my Rite in the sacred forests, like generations of Blacks before me, was something that had not even crossed my mind. "Perhaps, the summons is not about the Rite," I told her.

She didn't reply.

I had never been inside the palace. Seeing how richly decorated it was made me feel small and out of place. Statues of lavish marble filled the halls, banquet tables were laden with golden bowls that overflowed with fresh, succulent fruit that looked even better than the very best sold at our humble market.

We were about to remove our masks when we were stopped by two of the elders' servants. Although both were dressed and masked in the same way, they couldn't have been more different. One was tall and gaunt while the other was short and stout. Both had checkered black and white masks; the tall one with an exceedingly long nose, the short one with bulging cheeks.

"Bumpkins!' the tall one shrieked at us, "this is a sacred place! You will keep your masks on and remain in silence until you are called upon."

"In silence!" repeated the other.

And so we waited. The vigils passed and with them a flurry of chromes that came to attend to this or that elder. No one acknowledged our presence. I looked at my mother from time to time, but dared not talk to her. She stood still, staring at a point on the opposite wall. Her cloak rustled as she trembled. Looking back now I know that by the time the chrome with the black mask, not dressed as elegantly or richly as an elder, made his way through one of the halls to speak with the tall servant, she already knew why we were there. The servant pointed toward us and this new chrome hastened over.

He faced my mother, cleared his throat and said: "Your husband has died in battle, sister. The nation and the gods will not forget his sacrifice." He spoke as if he was in a big hurry, delivering news of my father's death as if discussing a new law, without any words of consolation or gratitude.

For a moment, I remained dumbfounded. Surely he was speaking of someone else, not of my father? My father could not die, he was a great warrior. He had won two great wars.

My mother remained in silence. I felt her hand look for mine and then grab it tightly. For a moment it seemed she would falter, but it was only a moment.

"Are you sure?" she finally managed to say.

The Chrome nodded.

I wanted to know more. I needed to know. How many enemy soldiers had my father killed? How had he had died? I felt sure that his death had been brave, courageous, glorious. I needed to hear it. But after giving us notification, it was clear that to the black masked chrome we were no more than an inconvenient nuisance he wanted to dismiss as quickly as he could. It was surely not possible for things to get worse in that moment. But then they did. As he made to leave, he turned back to us and said in a prim, condescending tone: "I must remind you that to talk of a soldier's death in public during wartime is considered an offense to the gods. And the elders take the offense to the gods very seriously."

That was it. He left without saluting us. Moments later, the servants were ushering us out of the palace. My mother did not say a word until we reached our home. There, she took off her mask and hugged me, hard, almost suffocating me. Afterward, she went into her room, closed the door and screamed like I had never heard her scream before. I was confused, devastated and angry; angry at my father for getting killed, for leaving me and my mother alone; for not being the invincible chrome I always thought he was.

Hora, the god of time, now made the days longer than the nights. After an eternity, the city was filled once again with the scent of budding flowers which perfumed the breeze. Spring had arrived. In other times, this would have marked the beginning of the hunt, when my father and I would go outside the walls to hunt for boars and deer. We loved exploring new places in the woods, where he would teach me forest craft and hunting skills. It was the times I remembered him at his happiest. He was never like that inside the walls. I missed him. The pain of my loss was physical and intense; a burning hole in my heart that felt like it would break me.

Now I was the one to gaze upon my friends with bitter envy. Why were their fathers still alive instead of mine? Why did my father have to be in the First Army? I asked some of my friends about when their fathers would be going to the front, but they said their fathers had to stay behind because of the services they rendered to the elders. What those services consisted of, I never found out. I could not understand why, in time of war, some chromes stayed home and others were called to arms. I experienced something I had never known up to that point in my life. A feeling of injustice.

Our days at the seminary became ever harsher, our training and preparation rituals more intense. Rumors spread that we were being readied to go to war ourselves even before the Rite. But then, as was often the case, the gods decided for us.

One day, after sunset, the Orator did not appear on top of the palace stairs. A large crowd of worried chromes made their way to the square after news of his absence spread.

My mother, in her purple mask of mourning, had still come every day and listen to the Orator, even though the war should have not mattered to her any longer. I reluctantly accompanied her. It was as if she was hoping that one day he would deliver the news that my father was still alive and on his way home. But unfortunately, that would never be. As for me, the war reminded me of my father and the less I heard of it, the better.

On this particular day, the square was bursting with worried, angry chromes. "We want to see the Orator!" a few of them near us, shouted.

"Elders come out!" cried others.

Then, as the red moon began to swim across the sky, the Eldest finally came out of the palace, followed by his guards. He stood at the top of the stairs and waited for hush to settle over the restless crowd.

"Devout sons and daughters of the Black nation," he began, "tonight is a sad night for us. The Red kingdom has annihilated our entire First Army. The Second and Third Armies are retreating. The God of fate has chosen its winner and it is not the Black nation."

Now the crowd began to shout in disbelief. I could hear many crying. Others angrily cursed the gods for taking sides against us, their chosen ones.

"What will happen now?" shouted one chrome.

"The Red kingdom has annexed the Forests of the East" said the Eldest, his voice tinged with a hesitancy and shame I would have scarcely thought he was capable of. "They are no longer Black territories."

A roar of dismay arose from the crowd. The Eastern forests were sacred to the Blacks and the fact that the Reds had annexed them was a brutal humiliation. Our hatred for the Reds could only increase.

"They can't take them!" screamed a female voice. "The forests represent the birth of the Black nation!"

Others murmured similar concerns until the two guards standing beside the Eldest shouted for us to be silent, punctuating their order with loud thumps with their spear shafts on the steps.

"We have no choice!" said the Eldest. "The Red army will march towards our city and siege our walls by tomorrow's red moon rise if we don't accept their terms. Is that what you want?"

No one replied.

"There will come a time for revenge," continued the Eldest. "But for now, we must accept the unacceptable."

The sound of weeping spread across the crowd, from both female and male chromes. I had never before witnessed or felt such intense misery and despair. But worse was to come.

"That is not all," continued the Eldest. "Each family must give ten ounces of gold as compensation to the Red families who have lost their members during the war."

Now chromes began to shout and protest in earnest. "We have no such amount!" came the cries.

"Then you will take it from the gold of your best masks!" the Eldest replied. I was angry at how harsh and impatient his voice sounded.

"What about our husbands?" I heard someone else yell. It was my mother. "Who will compensate us for such loss? Who will compensate our sons for growing up without their fathers?"

The crowd roared their approval at her words and the guards had to struggle to silence everyone again.

"Your husband and all our valiant soldiers will be compensated by the gods," said the Eldest.

"And what kind of gods would let us lose our most precious land and our most valuable chromes? Our gods have abandoned us!" my mother cried.

"My patience is running thin, female chrome!" sniffed the Eldest. "Do not provoke the gods any further. We will all do as the Red kingdom has instructed. Tomorrow, at the second vigil of the sun, each family must bring the gold. That is the price to pay for our lives."

Back at home, when my mother took off her mask, I saw an expression that I had not seen on her face in a long time: her resignation had given way to resentment and anger. "Wrath of the Gods!" she repeated several times. "If your father and the rest of the legionaries had been here, the Eldest would not have been so arrogant." She went to her room and slammed the door closed behind her.

"Maybe the Elders are angry too," I replied out loud so she could hear me. "For not being able to protect us."

The door to her room opened slowly. Behind it, the pale face of my mother, holding a candle.

"And who will protect us from them, Asheva?" she said before blowing out the candle.

I went to sleep hoping that things would soon be better for us. But the howling wind made my sleep difficult. In my dreams I saw the crowd at the palace and heard a loud, insistent banging.

After a moment I realized that I was dreaming and the banging was real.

I opened my eyes. Someone was banging at our door in the middle of the night.

My mother came rushing out of her room with a finger on her lips.

The door banged again.

"Open the door!"

That voice. I had heard it before and would recognize it anywhere.

My mother nodded as I slowly opened our door. The Eldest was standing outside, with his long cloak dancing in the wind.

"It's about time," he said entering.

Surprised and awed by his presence, I bowed low and stood back to let him pass.

"I see you are growing up to be strong like your father," he said as he took off his mask. I was now even more astonished. I had been expecting a man of advanced years, but his face was that of a chrome in his prime. He had ice blue eyes and dry, dull hair like dead leaves. "Our nation needs young chromes like you," he added. I bowed again, this time flattered.

My mother was just as stunned to see him. She struggled to compose herself and control the unhappiness this unusual visit inspired in her. "Why do you choose to honor us with a visit to our home…" she asked, placing some customary cheese and honey on the table, "… Your Grace?"

Although she was still angry from the night before, I could not help but be enthralled to have the Eldest in our house and feared he would be offended by the strained, hostile tone of her voice. But if he picked up on any enmity or disrespect, he dismissed it. Instead, he sat down at our table, in what used to be my father's seat, and began to eat, keeping an amused eye on my mother.

"You should try to quell your temper," he said after a while. I understand these past months have been hard for you both. But these are difficult times for all, not just for you. There are chromes who conspire against us. We must be very careful in separating friends from foes." He stared at her, his eyes piercing hers. "Very careful."

My mother's eyes widened. This only happened when she became angry and I braced myself for a tirade. But it didn't come. Instead, she cast her eyes downward in what looked like a show of deference and respect. "I understand. And beg forgiveness," she said. My mother was a proud female chrome. I had never heard her apologize to anyone, not even to my father. I knew something was wrong.

The Eldest for his part, seemed to appreciate her muted behavior. "Good," he said. "But that is not the only reason why I am here. I have a proposition to make."

Now he looked at me, "On my way here, I smelt the sweetest, fresh smelling bread one can imagine. The market - is it close?"

I nodded.

"Then do me a favor, young chrome," he said, producing a silver coin. "Go and fetch us some."

I glanced at my mother, not about to go anywhere without her say-so. She hesitated and I noticed a strange sadness in her eyes. A different sadness from the one she expressed for my father.

She nodded. "Go Asheva." I remained still. She hastened to my side, urging me to leave: "Go on, I'll be all right."

Reluctantly, I took the coin and went outside. A short way along the alley stood two guards. By their masks I recognized them as being from the Eldest's own protection cohort. The wind was still blowing hard like a banshee as I made my way towards them. The branches of the trees seemed to have come alive like a thousand arms swinging wildly towards me, as if they were trying to prevent me from taking one step further towards the market. Maybe it was the way of the gods to warn me, but as the guards glanced up to see me, I turned in to a small passageway leading off the alley and down the hill. After making sure I hadn't aroused the guards' suspicion in any way, I climbed over a wall in to the yard of our neighbors' house and then over another to come out on a narrow pathway that ran up to the back of our house. I moved up to the back door and, making sure my footsteps were as silent as a catkin's I pushed it ajar to see if I could sneak a look at the goings on, inside.

Our communal room was empty, and my father's chair was down on the floor. I heard my mother's wracking sobs coming from her bedroom. With a lump rising in my throat, I crept toward her room and put my eye up to the crack of the door. Through it, I saw her standing by her bed, cringing, disgusted, while the Eldest ran his lips over the back of her neck and shoulders. My blood boiled. All I could think of was how he was so clearly enjoying her suffering!

There are certain events that take place in our life which have the power to ravage the rest of it; crossroads where choosing one direction instead of another changes our path forever. This was such a moment. In an instant I would be forced down a road I never imagined I'd tread. It would mark the end of the life I had known and the beginning of my life as an adult chrome...

4. The Eastern Gates

My mothers' tears came from her soul. Her misery and pain were all too obvious and clear. In the heart of any normal, compassionate being they would have inspired sympathy and compassion. But not in the Eldest's. "You can't mourn him forever, Valia," he hissed in to her ear.

"No!" she sobbed. 'Please'.

He forced her down onto the bed and pinned her down. The sound of her sobbing and the sight of him tearing at her clothes triggered a fury inside of me that until then I had never known. An ancient Black proverb, spoken in my father's voice, rang through my mind. 'Blessed are the sons of departed warriors, for their swords will be their fathers' revenge.'

I burst in to the room and made for the eldest. I grabbed a hold of him and pulled him off my mother, hurling him to the floor. He sprang to his feet and turned to me, his eyes aflame.

"Leave now. And I might just think about

sparing your life."

"No," I heard myself reply.

"Asheva" said Mother, through terrified, breathless sobs. "Do as he says!"

I held the Eldest's seething gaze, returning it with all my defiance. Looking back now, I must have been terrified, but I don't think I gave myself time to even think about it.

"I'm not going anywhere." I said.

Which is when the Eldest reached in to his robes and pulled out a dagger. What happened in the next few short moments remains an indistinct fog of images in my mind. The Eldest rushed at me with the dagger. I dropped a shoulder and ducked out of its path. As the dagger flashed past, the Eldest lost his balance and fell stumbling to his knees. He was back up on his feet in an instant and coming at me again, thrusting the blade towards my heart. I can only think that my Rite training had sharpened my reflexes, my survival instincts. I stepped back out of the way and this time as the dagger moved past me I grabbed a hold of it by the handle and twisted it out of the Eldest's grip. He spun at me and tried to wrest it back again. As we tussled and grappled with one another, my Mother tried to get between us.

"Asheva!" she cried.

Powered by fury and with a great bellowing roar, the Eldest wrested the dagger away from me and slashed at Mother with it, catching her on the side of the face, drawing blood. The sight of it arrested him for just a moment and propelled me to another height of rage and affront. In one motion I snatched the dagger from his grasp again and plunged it as hard and as deeply as I could in to him. It slid in to this ribcage. As his eyes widened with disbelief, I yanked it out again and then stabbed him in the stomach, over and over again. In a frenzy of rage and affront I continued until I was sure his soul had finally departed his flesh.

The Eldest's lifeless body slumped to the floor with a heavy thud, my knife still in him. My mother gripped the blade's hilt. It slid out of his body with a sucking sound. She pressed her hands against his wounds, but she couldn't staunch the blood. The bedroom resembled a slaughter house. There was blood everywhere, over the sheets, over our clothes, over the walls, the floor and even in splashes across the ceiling.

A shrill cry pierced the stillness. At first I had no idea where it came from. Then I realized it came from me.

I saw the Eldest's blood drip from my fingers and felt its sticky warmth. I heard my mother's hacking sobs. I was crying too, but my tears were not of sorrow or remorse; they were a farewell to my youth. Before I could even begin to grasp the magnitude of what I had done, Mother was already moving to act. She rose and wiped away her tears which now mingled with blood.

"Your face,' I said.

"I'm fine," she replied.

I went to the window and glanced out. The two guards were still at their posts at the end of the alley. But it wouldn't be long before they would be expecting the Eldest to reappear. When he didn't, they would come looking for him. Mother was already gathering up a robe and various items of my clothes from a cupboard, shoving them in to a canvas bag. Her movements were steady and precise, not panicked at all; as though she were in a daze.

"You have to go," she said while wiping the blood off me.

"Both of us" I said.

"No-"

"I'm not going without you."

"I'll say it was me-"

"No."

"Listen to me, Asheva-"

"They'll kill you!"

"My life is over, anyway. It ended the day your father died."

She took my face in her hands.

"You must live, do you understand me? Or he died for nothing. Then they will use you as a scapegoat to take the minds off the loss of the war."

"But why?" I asked her.

"Because they're all the same, Asheva," she said. "Bad weeds grow in bunches." She nodded at where the Eldest lay. "His stem was just the tallest of the lot. But you still need to live, so you can become a great warrior, just like your father. One day, you will return to fight the injustice and the wrong that has been done to us."

"Where shall I go?" I asked.

"Far away" she replied, stroking my face. "As far as possible. Far enough that the guards will never find you."

I knew she was right. I had just killed our supreme authority; probably the worst sin I could have committed as a Black chrome. Mother prepared a sack with food and robes for me to take along. Then she opened a drawer and took a dagger from it, handing it to me. It was my father's. An ornate, carved wood handle below a sleek silver blade.

"Take this too," she said. "This way you will always remember him." Then she took off her medallion and placed it around my neck. "And me," she said. Taking some gold and silver coins from a casket under her bed, she pressed them in to my hand and said through tears: "May the gods protect you, Asheva."

I noticed the blood of the Eldest had stained the coins. I put on my black cloak and we hugged each other, both of us knowing it was probably for the last time.

The sound of voices outside brought us back to our dire situation. The guards were coming.

"Go!" said Mother. "Now!"

At first I couldn't move. All I could do was stand and look at her, hardly able to believe that it could be the last time I would ever set eyes on her.

"What will you do?"

She kissed me and held me tight one last time before leading me to the back door and all but pushing me out of it.

"Live long Asheva," she said and closed the door.

I ran for the wall at the end of the yard glancing back for the final time at the only home I had ever known. I yearned to stay, and for a moment I was tempted to open my door and go back inside, but I knew I couldn't trick Hora, the god of time. The deed had been done and I knew the gods' watchful eyes were upon me as they debated my fate. I hastened toward the main gates of the city, those same gates from which my father had left and never returned.

The sun rose beyond the city walls, but the streets were still deserted. As I slipped my way through familiar alleys, I heard the sounds of young and old alike attending to their morning chores. I could smell bread baking in the ovens. I was so lost in the misery of my own thoughts I didn't notice that my steps had taken me past Andahar's house. I bumped into him as he came out his front door, lugging an empty bucket.

"Whoa?" he said. "Where are you going this early?"

I had no time to think of any kind of convincing reply. So I simply stammered: "Er, nowhere."

"What d'you mean, nowhere? You're never up at this hour!"

"I meant nowhere special. Just to the seminary."

"And you were coming round to call for me, weren't you?" he said, with an enquiring smile. "Because you wouldn't sneak out by yourself to get a little extra practice in for the Rite, would you?"

I didn't know what to say. Standing there in front of him I was convinced I looked foolish, guilty, or more probably a combination of both. But I couldn't give anything away. I had to get rid of him. If the guards saw him with me they would think he was involved as well and the last thing I wanted was to get him in trouble.

"Andahar. I have to get going."

Now he seemed to sense that something was wrong.

"Is everything okay?"

"Yes, it's fine."

He looked at me for a moment before beaming at me once more. "Good. Wait there. I'll come with you."

"No!" I said, startling the both of us with my urgency and aggression. "I mean ... I have to go alone."

"Why?"

"I can't tell you."

"Why not?"

"Because I just can't, okay?" I hissed.

Now he looked concerned again. "Asheva, are you all right?"

Now he pointed at my sleeve, reaching out to touch it.

"You can't turn up at the seminary with stains all over your-"

He pulled up, because as he took his hand away, his fingers were smudged with blood. As he stood there looking at them, trying to make sense of what his eyes were telling him, I heard shouting and voices approaching along the alley behind me. Andahar looked at me, uneasiness in his eyes.

"What's going on, Asheva?"

I had no choice but to throw myself on the mercy of our friendship.

"You have to help me," I said, glancing back along the alley

Andahar followed my gaze to see the guards moving towards us.

"What have you done?"

"I can't tell you," I said. "But I need to hide. Please."

With clear unease, Andahar nodded me to follow him and headed towards his house.

"Go in behind the side gate. Don't let my parents see you."

I ran up the steps to the house and in through the gate. I crouched there and listened as the guards stopped and spoke to Andahar.

"Have you seen a young chrome come this way? Your age?

"I don't think so," I heard Andahar reply.

There was a pause, before the guard said.

"You don't think so? What does that mean?"

"I mean, no. No I haven't."

I heard the guards making their way off. Just as I allowed myself to breathe my relief, I heard Andahar call after them to ask them the one question I didn't want him to.

"What has he done?"

There was a pause, during which I prayed that the guard would tell my curious friend to mind his own business. But the gods' attention was clearly elsewhere at that moment.

"He has assassinated the Eldest."

I heard cries and shouts of horror go up along the road. Then the guard continued.

"The traitor's name is Asheva. Anyone who knows where he is and doesn't tell us will share his fate."

Andahar was my oldest friend. We had known each other since we were born. Was he ever going to believe what he had just been told? I would find out soon enough. A moment later, the gate opened and Andahar was there, his mask off, looking at me with an expression of disbelief and bewilderment.

"Is it true?" he asked.

I could only stare at him.

"I had no choice," I said.

It was as though I had seared his skin with a red-hot spear. He started back from me, shaking his head, an expression of revulsion and disgust transforming his face.

"How could you?" he said.

"Andahar, please try to understand-"

But he was already running back towards the alley, calling out after the guards.

"He's here! I've found him. Asheva the traitor!"

He turned back to me, with an accusing finger directing every gaze towards me. I turned and ran for my life. Reaching the end of Andahar's yard, I took the wall in one leap in to a narrow passageway which in turn led to a maze of even smaller and tighter gunnels and alleys I had known since I could walk. With the shouts and calls of my pursuers closing in from behind and then from all around, I took off deep into them. I can't recall how many turns I took, how many times I doubled back on myself or how many walls I leapt to evade the guards tracking me from every direction. I hid in a ditch, crawled under a bridge, and pressed myself inside a gap between two buildings as the guards moved past me, so close I felt the draught of them as they went.

Eventually, I came out from a side street where I could see a crowd of farmers and merchants gathered by the city gates with their carts of merchandise and their flocks of animals, waiting for the eastern gates to be opened. The eastern gates were the city's main entrance and had by far the largest doors of the fortified walls. They were made of heavy cast bronze, with each door as wide as three chromes and taller than four. At the seminary, they taught us that the bronze used for the doors had been taken from the spears of the first Black warriors upon their death. The doors were now engraved with their names.

A sundial near the gate tower displayed the first vigil of the sun. The bronze doors were about to open. A small queue of merchants and farmers ready to leave the city had already formed. I joined the back of the line while the guards poked through the belongings of the other chromes. Fear choked me. I tried to still the trembling in my legs and arms but the more I tried the more I could feel myself shaking. I hoped to all the gods that nobody would notice, but was convinced that everybody had. I was sure I could still smell the Eldest's blood on me, as if it had stained my body forever. I prayed, again, to the gods that the guards wouldn't ask me anything. I wouldn't be able to answer them if they did.

Then, to my relief a voice from up on the tower shouted: "Open the gates!" The two doors began to slowly swing open with a grating, metallic creak. The chromes in front of me moved forward while the sun's rays hit the walls of the buildings, bringing the bricks to life with colors of fire. For an instant, Axyum turned into a golden shrine, just like the sacred abode of the Gods.

"Where are you going?" A harsh voice broke the spell.

An imposing guard frowned at me. "You should be on your way to the seminary, not to the fields. And why are you wearing a mask of celebration? There is nothing to celebrate!"

In my haste, my mother had handed me my best mask, my black onyx one, instead of my everyday one. "Which family are you from?" The guard asked.

Before I could answer him, a gangly male chrome bolted past us, shouting: "The Eldest is dead! The Eldest has been murdered. The traitor is in the city!"

The guard's attention shifted to him. As the news rippled through the crowd, panic and confusion set in. The queue broke up. Even the guards surrounded the news-bringer, demanding to know more and threatening him with his life if he was lying. I slipped closer to the gates, unnoticed. But as I did, one of the senior guards called out to those who operated the huge wheel that cranked the gates open and close. "Close the gates!" As they started to creak and shut in front of me, I had to force myself not to break out into a run. To do so would only bring attention. The early morning sun's rays that fell in through the two brass gates narrowed before me. If I didn't run now, I wouldn't make it. I would be trapped. With a glance over my shoulder, I saw that everyone's attention was focused behind me. It was now or never. The gates would be closed in seconds. I had to risk it, I had to run. I picked up my pace and sprinted the last distance – hurling myself through the gates just as they ground shut. I paused to listen behind me for any shouts or calls of exclamation. Had I been seen? From the continuing hubbub and to my great relief, I guessed not.

But whatever positive feelings I allowed myself lasted barely any time at all before I was hit by a sudden and overwhelming sense of loss. I would no longer be part of this city and of my people. Everything I had ever known was about to be gone forever. I touched one of the gates with my hands in the hope that it would bring me good fortune and then I made my way downhill, never looking back.

A fertile valley spread out before me. There were fields ripe with golden wheat, red poppy flowers, violets and yellow sunflowers. The sparkling blue River Axi flowed through the valley, sewing all the patches of different color together like a living quilt. In the distance, I could see rolling green hills. Beyond them was the place where I cast my hope of survival. The mighty Eastern forest.

My descent from the city's hill seemed to take an eternity. Every heavy step was like slogging through mud. I was convinced that at any moment the guards would start shooting arrows at me from the tower behind. Still, I fought the urge to break in to run. If I did that, it might give anyone watching every reason to shoot at me.

My luck held: no one seemed concerned with any activity outside the walls; they were still too alarmed by what had happened inside them. So taking the opportunity of distraction, I dashed toward the first field of sunflowers that I came across and plunged inside it. It would provide a good cover as I moved farther away from the city.

As I pushed my way through the tall, thick sunflowers I heard the order to close the gates echo throughout the valley, sending a shiver through me. I thought of my mother. Were they closing the gates because she confessed instead of me? If so, what would happen to her? Did they think I was still hiding inside the city? Would she tell them the truth? Would she be imprisoned? Or worse, would she be hanged just like the harlequin I had seen? Then there was the Eldest. Would the gods seek revenge on me for what I had done? Would they take their revenge on my father who was in the heavens with them? The more such questions raced through my mind, the faster I ran, never stopping even once to catch my breath. The fear of seeing horse-guards riding after me was a strong and effective antidote to my fatigue.

After crossing more fields and streams than I could keep count of, I came to the end of the valley, where the hills began. Behind me in the distance, Axyum shrunk till it reminded me of the small wooden castles I had played with as a young child. When I reached the top of a large hill, I looked back to see great black flags whipping in the wind from the top of the towers. Waving farewell to me, I imagined. I turned and began my long hike through the hill country.

Up until then, my only concern had been to escape. I hadn't had time to think about the consequences of heading into the wilds alone. I had been to the forest many times before, but always with my father. "Follow the streams and rivers, Asheva," he used to say. "Water is life and life revolves around water. It will quench your thirst and quell your hunger."

The most powerful memories are those sparked to life by the senses. So the smell of damp earth and leaves and the scent of the trees that rose around me as I made my way through the woods recalled days spent hunting with my father. He only hunted what we needed to sustain ourselves – never for sport – and he made sure that we shared what we killed with the elderly of the city. This gave me a greater respect for the outdoors and wildlife. "Hunting for food will make you proud, and make you remember every single detail of the day you stalked your prey, Asheva," he said. "You must always thank and mourn the animal whose life you took. A chrome who takes pleasure in death just for death's sake is rotten somewhere inside. You'll see him do things later in life that prove it."

Some time later, I heard the sound of rushing water and did as my father had taught me. I followed the sound until I found the River Axi and then walked its bank to a narrow gorge. By this time, my long day had completely surrendered to darkness and I decided to rest. I got down on my hands and knees, took my mask off and drank deeply. Then I took the food in my sack and ate a quarter of everything. I found a log for shelter and I lay down with my head turned up to the heavens, trying to chart the different constellations my father told me about, but I couldn't concentrate. The day's events rushed in to haunt me.

I experienced my mother's despair all over again; in my mind's eye I saw the Eldest's malevolent smile. How could he be so evil? He was our supreme guide – the conscience of the Black nation and yet, in our house, he had acted like a scavenger feeding on the weak or the dead. He had tainted my family's honor and I was glad to have made him pay for it. I wondered if the other elders were like him? And what of the Headmaster? Had he inflicted pain on us for our own benefit or for his pleasure? Rage boiled up inside me. I was glad I wouldn't be attending the Rite to find out.

The wind picked up, rustling branches and leaves all around me and transforming them into looming gatekeepers of an evil kingdom. Everything seemed to breathe in unison with the sounds blending into a symphony that would have pleased an audience in the underworld. And that's when I heard the howl of wolves!

From the youngest age, Black chromes are told terrifying stories about the wolves of the Eastern forest. The size of an adult chrome, they would attack our city when the cold skies made Thiyria, the earth goddess, curl up under her mantle of snow to sleep away the winter. Occasionally, city guards found the ravaged remains of some poor chrome scattered around the walls. One time, a pack of them chased a shepherd and his flock back towards the gates. For fear of the wolves making their way through, the guards were ordered to close them before he could get through. Stories spread around the city for weeks and months afterwards of how everyone watched from the towers as the beasts tore apart this poor, wretched soul before feasting on his sheep.

Most of the time, however, the wolves stayed away from our city, finding easier prey in the wild. But now it was I who had invaded in their territory. I scrambled to my feet to search for a safe place to hide, while the words of my father now sounded like a terrible omen: "Staying close to the water will not only quench your thirst but also quell your hunger." Perhaps the wolves instinctively knew this as well.

5. Astor

The first howl was followed by a second, and the second by a chorus of calls and responses. There was a huge pack on the prowl, out there and getting close to me. Picking out an oak tree a few rods away from the river shore, I grabbed my sack and ran for it, hoping the beasts had not scented me. For now, I was down wind but that could change at any moment. I heaved myself up the oak's gnarled trunk, until I reached its main boughs. Just as I did, I heard the sound of leaves crunching on the forest floor below me. I held my breath. Wolves can hear better than any chrome. Any movement would have surely given me away, if it hadn't already.

I studied the ground spread out below me: the river to my left, the bank in front of me, and the woods to my right, bordering the oak tree. Pressed flat against the tree trunk, straining to hear what the forest had to tell me, the only sound I could hear came from the river as it ran through the gorge.

It seemed that all the wild creatures of the woods had the same intent; each one listening for and fearing the other. It was as if the earth goddess had decided to call a truce amongst her minions, because the silence lasted longer than any I had ever heard in the wilderness. Then an owl hooted. Maybe the wolves had gone elsewhere?

An intense tiredness from the long day washed over me. Snuggled between the oak's strong boughs, I started to shut my eyes. Not wanting to fall asleep, I snapped them open but within moments they began to close once more. Moments later they were wide open again as a surging bolt of fear shot through me. Something was moving below me.

Dark shadows emerged from the forest, swiftly making their way over to the river, their stealthy silence more disquieting than a thousand screams. I had dreaded being stalked by wolves, but now I knew the gods had a far worse punishment in mind.

The Black guards had found me.

I could pick out their silver masks in the gloom. Some held spears, others swords. The stories told by the Messenger were condescending, cautionary tales. This was real. They weren't hunting down an unknown Red, they were coming for me.

Sweat beaded on my forehead and my heart beat so loudly I was convinced the guards could hear it. I counted seven of them. One circled the trunk of my oak, studying the disturbed mud around it. All he had to do was turn his mask upwards and he would spot me. I heard one of the others say "the youngster has to be close by. He can't have gotten far."

It's one thing to imagine what it might be like to be prey, but it's another to experience it. My entire body began to tremble even as my grip on the bough tightened. Completely at the mercy of my hunters, I closed my eyes and prayed that the Supreme God might turn me into one of the branches so that no one could ever take me away from there. The guards would force me down and sink their spears and swords in to me. I would die a painful and terrible death away from my city, from my house, from my mother. Or worse yet, they would bring me back to Axyum to push me off the highest tower, leaving my remains beneath the walls to rot in the sun and be picked apart by wild scavengers.

Forcing myself to stay calm, I looked up above me, searching for a path further upward. As I did, I noticed a great number of Fieldfare birds roosting in the branches of the surrounding trees. They nested in groups, which was part of their defense against intruders. One of their most potent weapons, as I had learned at my expense during hunts with my father, was their excrement. When startled, Fieldfares flew out from trees and released their droppings copiously. Hoping to all the gods that I could still do it as well as my father had taught me, I did my best to mimic the Fieldfare's cry of alarm.

The results were immediate and spectacular. The squawking birds flew off and performed as expected. Shouts of horror and disgust from below put a temporary end to my misery, forcing the guards to continue their search elsewhere. Thanking the gods for my deliverance I climbed down from the tree and made off in the opposite direction to the Guards, despite it meaning going deeper in the forest where the Reds might still be lurking.

As the guards' voices faded away, my mind began to unhinge in the darkness. I was no longer sure where I was, or even if it was night or day. At one point, I could have sworn I heard my mother calling to me from across the river. I had turned to follow her voice when I stumbled over something and fell. Getting to my feet and looking down, I saw a body lying on the rocks, its head missing. My mind was still trying to make sense of the grotesque sight when I saw the head lying a little distance away. I recognized my father, his eyes staring wide and lifelessly at me. I choked down a scream and backed away, tripping over some roots. As I lay there I forced myself to look again. My mind had used my exhaustion to torment me. The dead chrome was a soldier of the First Army, but it wasn't my father.

The smell of death stung my nostrils. I ran, but the corpses seemed to be everywhere, scattered like logs across the floor of the forest. I had stumbled in to the scene of a massacre! As I ran, I tripped over more bodies, some of them whole and some in piece. I would get to my feet and run on only to fall over yet another. There was nothing of the glorious scenes of battle the Messenger had painted for the citizens of Axyum. This was a macabre theater of ghosts. On I went, running, stumbling and getting to my feet again. I thought I would never find my way out, but at length I made my way in to an open glade near the river.

"There he is. He's over here!" a guard shouted from behind me in the trees. "This way!"

I could run no more. Exhausted, I fell to my knees and asked the gods to let my death be swift. Now other voices joined in the commotion. Then I heard distant screams. At first, I thought they were killing an animal, but then I realized, to my horror, that the cries came from another chrome. And in that moment, my senses abandoned me. Everything became confused. I thought I heard the wolves again. They were close and getting closer, but I couldn't force my legs to work so that I could get up and run. I think I saw the wolf pack pass me by, although it could have just been my fevered and fractured imagination tormenting me.

Time passed, I have no idea how much. When I opened my eyes again, the sun had risen and the day was warm. I fully expected to see the silver glint of Black nation guard masks appear over me, but the only thing I saw as I glanced around me was a squirrel. As I began to test and move my limbs, he nimbly jumped from branch to branch until his lush, flashing tail was the last part of him to disappear into the forest.

My limbs were stiff and cramped from the night, but at least I could move again. I got slowly to my feet and walked towards the river, glancing about me all the while, still fearing an ambush from the guards. The current was stronger here and I spotted a mysterious pile of dark cloth on the shore, battling against the force of the water to reclaim it. As I moved closer, I realized that that this pile contained the body of a chrome.

He was tall, with long, dark hair. Even though his face was badly bruised, his body seemed strong and well suited to endure hardship. He was older than me but younger than my father. He wasn't a guard; that much I could tell. A soldier perhaps? No, he wasn't wearing any armor.

Recalling the events of the night, pieces began to fit together. It must have been this poor unfortunate who the guards had found and chased down, unleashing their wrath upon him. His were the screams I'd heard. It hadn't been a dream at all. I looked down at him now with a growing sense of guilt and sorrow. It was I that should be laying here, not him. He had been forced to pay the ultimate price for my sins. I would pray to the gods for the safe journey of his soul, but I knew that he could not be accepted in to the heavens without a proper rite. Under any other circumstance, I would not have thought twice about making a funeral pyre but every moment I delayed putting as much distance as I could between myself and Axyum, the danger increased. The Black guards' thirst for vengeance would not be quenched until they found me. I had to move on – now– without looking back, just like Mother told me.

I gazed at the body beside me, once more. Perhaps I could move it into the current and let the river decide his fate? This much I owed him. But just as I leant down to him, his eyes fluttered open and he fixed me with a glazed stare. "Help...me." The words were clear even if his voice was feeble.

A cry of shock caught in my throat as for a moment, I thought that his soul had returned from the heavens. But no, he was really alive! I took out my mask from the sack and placed it on my face so he would not be able to identify me. Then, with panic suddenly setting in I scrambled away from him.

"Help me!" he said again. This time, his voice was no longer a whisper. I couldn't leave him like that. The gods would punish me if I did not act.

I began to help him out of the water. He was heavier than me and his drenched clothes made it more difficult, but I was able to drag him over to a dry rock and prop him up in a sitting position. In the sun, I realized that the dark cloth he wore was not black but green.

"That's better," he spluttered, between furious bouts of coughing up water. When his breath returned he studied me for a minute or two. "Who are you?" he asked.

"They call me Asheva," I said, immediately wishing that I hadn't.

"A young Black chrome, eh? I bet you were the one they were looking for?" He then coughed again.

He knew I was a fugitive. Think Asheva, I told myself, desperate to come up with an explanation that was simple and believable. "I'm looking for my father!" I replied. "I have to go! I cannot stay and help you."

"Wait!" he said raising his arm. "I can take you where they won't find you."

I stared at him and then back at the woods. I could just run away and leave him to his fate. Then again, I had no sense of direction, no idea where I could run to. For all I knew, I could run in circles until

I found myself face to face with the Black guards once more.

"I can't feel my legs, let alone use them properly" he said with a grimace of pain on his face. "If you leave me here, I will be easy prey for the wolves."

I had forgotten about the wolves. He was right of course; they would certainly sniff out this loot.

"Help me and I shall help you," he added. "You have my word."

"What do you want me to do?" I asked.

He pointed towards a dead tree trunk, stranded on the shore, not far from where we were. "Can you move that trunk into the river?" I was ready to do anything so long as it took me farther away from the guards. I ran over to the trunk and tugged hard. It was heavy, but luckily the water aided me and after a moment or so I was able to dislodge it from where it had stuck and move it along, careful not to let it drift to the middle of the river, where the current was strongest.

I helped the Chrome pull himself on to straddle the trunk and then hopped on behind him, relieved it was large and buoyant enough to hold us both. Once we were firmly on board this uncomfortable wet hunk of wood, we used our arms to paddle it into the middle of the river. As the tree was moved by the current, it picked up speed. A new thought occurred to me. "What if the guards see us from the woods?" I fretted.

"That's a risk we'll have to take," he replied. "At least the river doesn't leave traces."

"What's your name" I asked him. It took him a

moment to reply. "Astor," he said. "My name is Astor."

Why the hesitation? I wondered. Was that his real name? Why would he lie if it wasn't? These would have to be questions for another time. Right now I was only interested in getting to safety, wherever that might be. I looked behind me one last time, and a cold shiver ran down my spine. We remained silent for a long time, letting the current carry us swiftly down the river. I was still shaken by the events of the past day and he still suffered from the beating he'd received.

I did not know where the river led, although Astor was certain it would carry us away from the Black territories. He breathed with great difficulty which forced him to limit our conversation. Besides his name, the only other thing he told me was that he was a Green chrome.

I had never spoken to anyone who wasn't a Black chrome before. I did not know much about Green chromes. All I knew was that they were called the Nomad chromes because they did not have their own territories. They lived erratically, moving from one land to another, until chromes of other colors forced them away.

I finally took courage and asked him what the guards did to him.

"What should never be done to another chrome," he replied drily. "Fortunately, the Mother Goddess came to my rescue."

"Who is the Mother Goddess?" I asked astonished. "And how did she save you?"

"She is the protector of the Green," he replied. "She sent the wolves against those Black guards. And amidst the confusion, she led me to the river so that I could save myself. She might even have led you to me. Now, stay quiet and let me rest." As he said so, he lay down on the trunk and closed his eyes.

I had a thousand other questions for him, but he was asleep within moments.

The course of the river in the meantime, had taken us through lush vegetation. Luckily, the river bed remained large enough for our trunk to hold a steady course. The sun now rode high in the sky and dragonflies playfully followed our trunk on its downstream journey. My mood was anything but playful, though. We had mounted the trunk as if it were a horse, with one facing the other so that we could look in every direction and spot danger quickly. My back still ached from the night before. Even worse, our legs were halfway submerged in the chilly water. It was not a fun ride.

"Are you cold?" I finally asked, hoping to wake Astor up. He stopped snoring, but he did not reply. "My feet are cold," I said, this time louder.

"Then talk," he muttered, still half asleep. "Talking will keep your mind off your feet." Then, seeing that I had kept quiet, he spoke again. "Tell me what you did to run away like this."

I remained silent.

"Fine," he said. "Keep thinking about your cold feet then."

Not much time passed until he spoke again.

"Did you steal from someone?" he asked. I

shook my head. "Did you offend someone?" I shook my head again. "I killed someone."

Astor's eyes flicked open and his pale face lit up. He looked up at me from the base of the trunk and smiled.

"Really? That's interesting. I think I'd like to hear about that," he said. So I told him. I told him my entire story, right up to the events that led to our meeting. Astor remained silent throughout, absorbing every word. When I finished, I was afraid he would think of me as a dangerous fugitive and throw me in the river. Instead, in spite of his bruises he broke into a wide grin. "Served him right!" he said, meaning the Eldest. "You did what you had to do."

"Really?" I asked astonished.

"Of course! You defended your dignity and your mother's. The Mother Goddess was surely there to assist you."

I pondered his words for a while, without saying anything. I had not expected him to be very understanding. I began to like the Green chromes. "What is your Mother Goddess like?" I asked.

Astor took a deep breath and then began to speak as if he were the teacher and I the student: "She is in everything we do. She is in the air we breathe, in the river that flows. She is the supreme goddess; the one that created everything. The one that created us Green."

"I don't know much about the Green," I admitted.

"The sky is our shelter and the woods are our home" he said, smiling proudly. "We are the true descendants of the Mother Goddess, and her favorite."

He then explained that it was not true that the Green had been forced out of their territories to lead an erratic and nomadic life. "On the contrary," he boasted, "it is us Green that chose this, leading a free life, going from territory to territory, just as the gods intended it to be lived."

Astor told me that the Collective Laws were, in fact, the laws of nature as given to the chromes by the Mother Goddess.

"But then in time, the chromes in the cities began to erect walls against her, turning against her, instead of embracing her spirit."

He told me that Green chromes were not used to wearing masks and that it was the other chromes, notably the Black, which had forced them to use it. I had never heard anyone speak openly of such blasphemy and I wanted to counter his words with the truth I had learned in lessons at the seminary, but nothing would come out.

Nevertheless, my growing irritation must have been quite obvious, for Astor was once again quick with his tongue: "My young friend, your mask does not allow you to breathe the air fully. It does not allow you to see the beauty of the goddess of nature fully. Or taste fully. Or hear fully. It does not allow you to appreciate what beauty the goddess of nature has bestowed upon us all."

"The Collective Laws say we need to wear a mask!" I replied, still offended.

"Feh! The Collective laws weren't created to protect chromes, but rather to imprison them. That is why the Green live outside of the cities, away from their hypocrisy."

"But how do you live?" I asked. Astor shrugged. "I live with whatever gifts the Mother Goddess is generous enough to bestow on me, my friend."

As the sun began its slow descent from the sky, I could hear the roar of a waterfall in the distance. We needed to get ourselves off the river, and quickly. We frantically paddled toward shore, fighting rapids as we went. The roar of the waterfall grew and grew until it filled our ears. As we got nearer to the bank I jumped in to the water and pushed the trunk. It was difficult at first and I swallowed great mouthfuls of water which nearly choked me. But as the water grew shallower I could walk and with Astor helping me as much as he could with his arms, we finally beached the log on the bank. I looked beyond the river, out onto the vast plains which opened below the falls.

"The Blue Plains!" Astor cried.

They may have been called the Blue Plains, but to me they looked like a golden sea, full of wheat, as far as the eye could see. It undulated in the wind, just like waves. "This is where the Black nation gives way to the Blue territory," he added. "The guards won't look for you there."

I gazed out at the horizon, flooded by a sense of relief. I had made it out of the Black territory! But the relief soon made way for a troubling thought. I may have been safe, but my mother wasn't. For a long moment, I stood looking back at the forest, hoping to see her come out from the woods. Though reason told me to keep going, but my heart told me I would never be free until she was free.

I glanced towards Astor, who seemed to be in a brighter mood. He began to feel his legs again and with my help, he took small, limping steps. We decided to stop for the night as the sun was retreating behind the hills and we were both exhausted from the day spent on the river. We lit a fire and together we ate the few rations I had left in my sack, combining them with some berries I plucked from thorny brambles at the river's edge. Given his newfound joviality, I asked him where he was headed.

"The Harvest Faire," he told me.

"What is that?" I asked.

He widened his eyes. "You never heard of the Harvest Faire?"

I shook my head, embarrassed.

"The Harvest Faire," he explained, in an excited voice, "is the most important faire of all the territories! Chromes come from every land and journey to make commerce there."

"And where exactly is this Faire?" I asked intrigued.

"In Ayas of course! The city of the Blue chromes."

He went on to explain that the Blue chromes thrived on commerce and held the most important fairs for all sorts of wares: precious stones, silks, spices, metals, grains, wood. Anything you needed, you could find in the Blue plains. Ayas was the wealthiest city not only in the plains but in all the territories! The Harvest Faire coincided with warm days given by the

Mother Goddess, but chromes of every region also benefitted from her generosity since travel was made easy. Chromes came from far and wide to trade, hoping to make good profits.

"What do you sell in at the Faire?" I asked with a growing curiosity.

"Anything and everything," he replied. "I'm a tradesman." He gamely tried to smile even though portions of his face still resembled crushed fruit. "The secret is to buy low and sell high."

"But you have no merchandise" I pointed out. I assumed that, because of me, he had lost everything.

"I pick it up as I go along," he replied. Then he continued to describe the faire. "The ones who earn the most from the fairs are the Blue chromes themselves. They are able traders and merchants and their lavish riches are envied by chromes of every other territory."

He looked at me and then added, "Except us Greens of course. We do not envy the Blues' riches for their possessions are nothing compared to the treasures the Mother Goddess shares with us."

Astor told me that even when the Blues went to war, they preferred to pay other chromes to fight for them, for fear of losing their precious commerce. "There's a famous proverb, where I come from," he went on, "It says 'better to have a Black chrome knocking at your door than a Blue chrome trading near your stall."

"Why?" I asked, irritated again. "What's wrong with us Black chromes?"

Astor began to laugh. "What's wrong with

Black chromes?" he repeated. I was really annoyed now. I didn't think that the Black nation should be food for sport, the target of such scorn and disrespect and I told him so. It only seemed to spur him on all the more.

"I'm sorry, my young friend, but everything is wrong with your nation. All the Black chromes think about is war, honor, and sacrifice to the gods. They are arrogant and they insist that all the other chromes follow their path."

The thought that the Black nation was not admired or worse, could be hated by other chromes had never dawned on me until then.

"Luckily the Red defeated the Blacks this time," he then added.

"But it was the Reds that declared war on us in the first place!"

Astor's eyebrows shot up in surprise. "And who told you that? That's not what they say in the other territories."

I was much confused. Surely now he was simply lying to me. How could Astor, a Green chrome, know the truth about my nation? How could he know about our traditions of honor and dignity, when everyone knew that the Greens were capricious chromes who always ran from their responsibilities? What did he know about the war with the Red kingdom? I concluded that matters concerning the Black nation were for Black chromes alone, so I decided never to broach this subject again with Astor, for he would never understand. But I couldn't afford to fight with him about it, either. "Tell me about Ayas," I said changing the subject.

"It is a large city, the largest of all the territories. And then there is the pyramid, at the very heart of it."

"The pyramid?"

"The Blue Pyramid, grand jewel of Ayas. The Blues built it at the center of their market. They hold the Harvest Faire around it."

I tried to imagine the many wonders of Ayas and looked up to the sky, where the stars were shining above us, like benevolent custodians of the night.

"Astor," I pleaded, "take me with you to Ayas. After all, it is the Mother Goddess that made us meet. You said it yourself."

Astor grinned, "And who am I to say no to the Mother Goddess?"

6. A New Mask

The next day, I woke with the sun, feeling more alive than ever and decided to bathe in the river. The sweet water cleansed not only my body but also my soul. I had freed myself from the demons of guilt and felt grateful towards Astor to whom I had confessed my burden without being judged. Thanks to his influence, my gratitude now extended to the Mother Goddess, whom I realized must have cast her protection over me after I escaped Axyum.

When I came out of the water, I found Astor busy carving a piece of wood, using my father's dagger as a tool.

"You took it from my sack!" I said, shocked.

"That I did," he replied. "I needed a mask. I cannot go to Ayas without one and I cannot make a mask without a knife. So I looked in your sack and, luckily, you had one handy."

"You could have asked me."

Astor looked up at me, the dagger gripped

firmly in his right hand. "You were in the river," he said, and went back to his work. Curious to see the result, I stepped closer. He was shaping the wood with surprising craftsmanship and I could see the personality expressed in his mask coming to life.

"Where did you learn how to do that?" I asked.

"I taught myself," he said. "The Mother Goddess gives you everything you need. Then all you need to do is make the best of it."

"If the Mother Goddess gives you everything, why is it that you need to go to the Faire?"

He laughed and said that occasionally even the Mother Goddess got distracted. The mask he was making, he explained, was typical of the Green tradition – using images found in nature as a further way to revere the Mother Goddess. Astor's mask symbolized the sun, with rays emanating from the forehead.

"Will you make me a mask, too?"

He seemed puzzled by my request. "Why would you want one?"

I admitted I was afraid that any Black chromes visiting Ayas might recognize me and force me back to Axyum with them. Astor shook his head. "A mask cannot change your chrome. Black you were born and Black you will remain."

"Please, Astor."

He looked at me for a moment before getting to his feet and going to the elm tree from where he had taken the first piece of wood. He cut another piece and returned with it. He worked quickly and the result was not as good as his first mask. Astor said it symbolized a lightning, but to me, the scratch carved in the middle of the mask seemed more of a mistake dictated by hurry. I tried it on and it was slightly small too. Nevertheless, I did not complain, for there is nothing more detestable than an ungrateful chrome.

Astor said, "We'll also have to do something about your cloak." He was right. A chrome with a wooden mask and a black stained mantle would have certainly attracted attention.

"Here, give it to me," he said. I took off my mantle and handed it to him, not sure how he was going to turn black cloth into green. He limped up towards the river. By the time I realized what he intended to do, it was too late. "Wait!" I yelled as he threw it in to the water.

I watched on helplessly as the cloak my mother made for me drifted towards the falls. Astor looked at me with a solemn expression on his face. Then, taking off his green mantle, he took my father's dagger and tore it in two. Handing me one of the two newly-fashioned robes, he said "fortune has blessed you, young 'Green' chrome. Today marks your entrance into the house of the Mother Goddess."

So began my new life as a Green, with an ugly scratched mask and a raggedy mantle. I don't think any other chrome had ever tried this kind of thing before. It felt so strange. Like the cloak torn in two, one part of me felt exhilarated while the other part experienced the numbing loss of a limb.

Although Astor did nothing to hide his perplexity, at least he went along with my strange plan. Of course, if anyone were to approach me about the Green ways, I wouldn't have known the first thing to tell them. I heaved a resolute sigh. It would probably only be a matter of time before an elder in the Blue city of Ayas studied my aura and saw that I was, in fact, a Black. I decided I would worry about it later. If there was something to be learned from my flight from Axyum, it was not to worry about the next sunrise because there was still the night to overcome.

"We need to leave here and march on," said Astor, interrupting my thoughts. "At the rate we're going, we'll be lucky enough to get to the Harvest Faire before it ends." He hobbled a few steps but then he was forced to pull up because of the pain.

"You can't walk like this," I said.

"You know some other way?"

"The river!" I replied. It flows through the plains. We'll just keep using it."

"It doesn't flow in the direction of Ayas," said Astor. "It swerves towards the Red kingdom." His eyes scanned the plains, as though searching for a solution. "Instead of heading straight for the city, I suppose we could make our way toward the Cancerian. It can't be more than a day's journey."

The Cancerian, he told me, was one of the great roads that ran the length of the territories, joining the kingdoms. It led from the twin cities of the Yellow and Orange chromes down to the Red kingdom and then further south, deep into the Blue plains until, after passing through Ayas, it veined off into smaller roads. Astor hoped that amongst the many chromes traveling that road, we might find one generous enough to take us to Ayas with them.

So we began our descent into the plains, walking slowly and stopping often for Astor to rest. In front of us, as far as the eye could see there was only wheat. The further we walked the more Astor's legs hurt him. Suddenly, he fell flat on the ground. I thought he'd taken a spill, but he gestured for me to do the same.

"What is it?" I asked. He put his finger to his lips. Then after a moment or so, he cautiously raised his head above the wheat stalks so that only a small part of his mask was visible in the field. I stayed low, fearing danger, but then my curiosity got the better of me and I raised my head as well, following the direction of Astor's gaze. All I could see were the heads of two horses as they bent and raised them to nibble on some grain. I didn't understand how they might pose a threat to us.

Astor was already crawling towards the horses. I followed behind him, careful not to make any noise. Every few rods he would stop and raise his head. When we got to within a few rods of the two animals I saw they were hitched to a wagon. I also heard someone cutting the wheat. Astor pulled out something from his mantle. It was my father's dagger. I had no idea what he intended doing with it, but as he moved closer, the two horses sensed his presence. They both began to snort and shake their heads.

"Whoa," came a voice. It was the farmer. I watched him step out from behind the wagon to calm the two beasts. "Easy, you two." If the horses were trying to warn him, it was too late, for Astor moved quickly. Before the farmer grasped what was happening, he had already cut the traces of the horse closest to him. He mounted it and galloped away from the wagon, over to me.

"Grab my arm!" He shouted.

All I wanted to do in that moment was run away, but watching the furious farmer chase Astor, I realized there was no alternative but to get on the horse and further bind my destiny to his. So I stood my ground as the horse sped towards me, determined to hold on to Astor, even if it was fated to be the last thing I would do in my life. I braced myself and when the horse reached me I grabbed the Green chrome's arm with both hands. Astor's pull was strong. Up I flew, arcing high up in mid-air; I spread my legs, then … Whomp! No one was more surprised than I to find myself seated firmly on the horse's back. Truth be told, I had never been on a horse before but it is amazing how much a chrome can adapt in times of dire need.

I heard something hiss past my ear. For a moment, I thought a serpent had slithered into my mantle during my crawl through the wheat field. It was only after I noticed the second arrow passing within a hand's breadth of my other ear that I realized the farmer had a bow. He took aim, but our horse bolted across the fields, out of range. Soon the farmer and his wagon were reduced to nothing more than twin tiny spots behind us.

Astor cried out joyfully, raising his right arm. "Ah-ha, we did it!"

"You stole a horse!"

"I gave it its freedom back!"

"But it was not for you to decide."

"Animals are creatures of the Mother Goddess, they are meant to be free! Why chromes continue to enslave them is beyond me."

I did not quite understand how taking a horse from another chrome and using it for our purposes translated into liberating the animal, but Astor became further convinced as the horse made its way through the wheat. Then, in a more conciliatory tone, he said, "Feel its strong muscles work like a machine under our rumps. How can you doubt that the Mother Goddess meant for this horse to be free, to run wild in these plains. We are but the instruments she used to achieve her task."

It was true that the horse now seemed at ease with us, galloping as if it had been yearning to run all day long. When we were sure we weren't being pursued, Astor stopped and we switched places, for his legs were feeling the strain of his actions.

I carefully took over the reins and following Astor's instructions, initially made the beast go on a slow trot. But I could still feel the horse yearning for more, so I let it pick up speed. "What are you doing?" Astor cried.

"Giving it what you told me it wants."

The wind whipped around us, like a long, sweeping cloak. I inhaled the warm, earthy scent of ripe wheat and for the first time since before my father had marched out of the city gates to his death, I felt a sense of joy. At that moment, I truly did feel as if I were one with Astor's wild Mother Goddess. As sinful as it was to even think this, riding that stolen horse gave me an exhilarating sensation I'd never experienced before. The gods had rewarded me with the keys to my own destiny! I caught myself laughing and, behind me, I could hear Astor laughing, too.

7. The Cancerian

The next day, we rode until the sun reached its highest point in the sky and the golden fields of wheat around us had turned to grassland. For perhaps the fifth time that day, I began to fret about my disguise. Surely any elder who happened to glance my way would see my real aura?

"Are there a lot of elders in Ayas?" I asked Astor.

"No. In fact there aren't any. The Blues have no elders," he replied.

I was astonished to discover that only the Black nation was ruled by elders. Ayas was ruled by 'barons', a class of chromes who controlled the lion's share of their commerce. Each baron ran the guild of their specific trade, like silk, grain, or metals. Astor didn't know how many barons there were in total, but he told me there were so many different types of trades in Ayas, there were probably just as many barons.

"Look at that, up ahead," said Astor, drawing

my attention to a dark line that snaked toward the horizon in front of us. As we drew closer, I began to make out a colorful army of merchants, farmers and crafters, all heading to the Harvest Faire. The last time I'd witnessed such a long column of chromes had been the day our Black warriors marched out of Axyum to battle the Red. The thought of my father made me blink back tears.

"What is it?" I asked him, working hard to put all thoughts of my father from my mind for the moment.

"It's the Cancerian," said Astor.

As well as chromes, the endless convoy contained carts, drays and enormous wagons pulled along the road by donkeys, horses, and cattle. I had never seen such an incredible display of merchandise in my life. There were crates filled with exotic silks, spices, and animal skins, finely crafted jars full of nectars and oils, and woven baskets heaped with dry fruit and salted meats. There were also bushels of harvested grain and wheat of different colors, some of which I'd never seen before.

Chromes, young and old, transported as much as they could carry on their backs. I could see many Red and Yellow chromes, but fewer Orange and Violet. Astor said there weren't any Blues as they rarely set foot outside Ayas. "They wait for others to bring goods to them. That's how powerful they are."

Astor and I seemed to be the only Green chromes walking the Cancerian, at least amongst the section of the crowd we ventured into. "Most Green will shy away from fairs," he said, his voice tinged with bitterness. "We are often unwelcome."

I scanned about me for Black chromes but did not see any. Perhaps we were also not welcome. There was so much I still had to learn about the territories. While it felt uncomfortable to find myself so close to Red chromes, especially knowing that one of them had killed my father, it gave me the chance to study them for the first time. All wore red mantles and most had silver or white masks with red ornaments covering their faces. Underneath their cloaks, they wore robes of white and red. I saw Orange chromes for the very first time, and was struck by the brilliant tangerine feathers adorning their masks and their robes of soft, calfskin brown suede and orange silk. Whilst all around me were strange new sights and sounds to absorb, it was the fruit and meat that made the biggest impression on me, or certainly on my stomach. The berries I'd eaten that morning had left me unsatisfied, and now my stomach was growling.

Our horse slowed to a trot behind an ungainly convoy. I felt around inside my sack for the coins my mother gave me, but couldn't find them. How could I have been so foolish as to lose her precious gifts? I tried to remember the last time I'd seen them. Was it in the oak tree? No, perhaps on the river? Fool, fool, fool! What will you do now?

"I'm hungry," I said to Astor.

"Me too," he replied whilst gazing all around us.

"I don't have any coins to buy food with," I added.

He turned to face me. "Sell your Black mask

then," he said unexpectedly. "That way we can both eat."

He was referring to my onyx mask, the one I kept hidden in my sack. My father had had it made for me by Axyum's most gifted artisan and it was the only thing that remained of my Black kin... How could I possibly part with it?

"Why would anyone want to buy it?" I asked.

"Because they can break the stone it's made of and use it again," replied Astor. Lowering his voice, he added: "and since you are no longer a Black chrome, you won't be needing it anymore, will you?"

That struck deep. Astor was right. I was no longer a Black chrome. His words sounded like a condemnation. I could not say that I was a Green chrome either, although I wore a Green's robes. So who was I? What was I going to become?

Astor, in the meantime, had made his mind up. Spurring the horse from a trot to a slow canter, we moved passed the motley convoy of chromes we had been following. "There's a merchant of masks a few rods in front of us," said Astor." I saw him before." Sure enough, amidst the dust and the animals, a sturdy horse pulled a trim red cart full of masks. A Red chrome was perched in the driver's seat.

We rode our horse until we pulled abreast of the cart, which was full of bronze masks; masks that I knew well. Masks my father and others of his Legion wore when they left Axyum for the last time.

"Greetings!" Astor cried out to the merchant.

The Red chrome turned to us. If the commerce of masks was a rich one, he surely was not profiting from it. His red robes, though clean, were old and worn. His mask was chipped and gray. It had probably been white at some stage. "Greetings," he replied, cheerful enough.

"This is a happy day for you my dear Red merchant, blessed by the gods."

"Oh yes? And why is that?' replied the chrome, warily.

"Because you have the chance to make the best trade of the day without even reaching Ayas!" cried Astor.

The Red chrome did not seem particularly impressed by Astor's words. He turned his gaze back to the road ahead.

"Quick, give me your onyx mask," Astor said to me.

At the insistence of my stomach, I did. "Take a look, O Merchant!" Astor said, raising the mask. "A fine and graceful black mask; finely crafted and entirely made of noble gemstone."

The Red chrome still did not seem interested, but we had captured the attention of other chromes, for this was an unusual location for trading.

"Afraid you'll only get a broken coin for it in Ayas, eh?" One of them guffawed out loud.

"Why don't you do your trading with the forest creatures, Green?" said another. "That's where you belong!"

Finally, the Red chrome turned towards us again. But rather than the mask, he seemed more concentrated on me, the owner.

"Three coins of bronze," he said.

"Three coins of bronze?" Astor repeated in disbelief. "Master Red, you must be mistaken. The sun has been beating down on your poor skull for too long. This mask is worth at least three coins of silver."

"I am sure he who owns it would think the same, but you are not he," the Red chrome replied.

"I am so!" I called at him without thinking. "And you are certainly not the owner of those bronze masks! They belong to the sons of the Black nation!"

Startled by my reaction, both Astor and the Red chrome stared at me. Neither one said anything, not sure how to act.

What's this?" another chrome traveler laughed. "A Green chrome that speaks like an emperor?"

"Get back in the woods, you filthy Green!" shouted yet another.

The Red chrome spoke again, pretending he'd never heard my words. "Three coins of bronze," he repeated. "No more, no less."

"Agreed," said Astor, handing him my black celebration mask and grabbing the three coins the Red threw back at us out of the air. We went on our way again, away from the merchant's cart and the chromes that had insulted and threatened us, back to where the carts full of food were. Astor turned to me, his eyes flashing with anger.

"Idiot! You almost gave yourself away!"

"I'm sorry. But he—"

"Don't ever act so stupid around me, again. I gave you my word I would help you and the Mother Goddess is my witness that I have kept it. But if you don't think before opening your mouth, you won't last long out here. The territories are dangerous grounds. If you don't believe me, try doing something like that again."

"I believe you," I said. Though I seethed for having obeyed my stomach rather than my brain. I was far angrier that I'd settled for so little from a scavenger of Black warriors, and for meekly submitting to a tongue lashing by a Green rogue. But Astor was right, I could not let my heart and gut rule my head and hope to survive. We ate what little we could buy with our three coins and pressed on. As the day drew to a close, we passed by many, different-sized pyramid shaped structures that lined the Cancerian.

"What are those?" I asked.

"Tombs," replied Astor. "Ayas does not bury its dead inside the city walls so the city is surrounded by burials. And as the city has grown, so have its burial grounds. As we get closer to it tomorrow, you'll see many more of these."

"Why the pyramids?" I asked.

"It's their symbol. The Blue Pyramid inside Ayas has brought the Blue chromes fortune and wealth, so Ayans hope that the same fortune can be brought with them to the heavens if their graves resemble it." Astor then raised his mask slightly and flashed me another one of his cocksure smiles. The Greens, he claimed, knew better. To meld with Mother Goddess was what truly brought a chrome eternal riches, beyond which nothing else could compare.

When night arrived, the entire caravan stopped, as if obeying an unwritten ancient law amongst travelers. The campfires lit throughout the road made the Cancerian seem like a long spear of light piercing the darkness.

      We stopped near a tree and tied up our horse. With the help of a few good-willed merchants, I crafted a torch so I could see my way around, while I hunted for firewood and horse fodder. I passed by several pyramid-shaped tombs. Most were constructed of fine, veined marble. Stepping closer to one of the more imposing monoliths I noticed some words engraved on it. I placed my torch next to the stones and began reading out loud:

> *Come and rest O wayfarer, near my tomb.*
> *My name was Sestertiu and though I was a*
> *shrewd merchant and able tradesman,*
> *All my wealth and all my power could not give*
> *me immortality.*
> *My heart was obscured by greed*
> *And my eyes were blinded by envy.*
> *Say a prayer for me before you resume your*
> *journey and know this,*
> *The only medicament to death is life, so live*
> *fully before your precious cure finishes.*

      I then passed a second tomb, and although it was much smaller than the first, it had a more amusing read:

> *To whoever shall dishonor my tomb or steal my*
> *ornaments,*
> *Think twice!*
> *May you and your descendants be cursed by ill*

fortunes,
And your life struck down by the will of the
Gods!
Listen to my advice!
Or your daughters shall never marry and your
sons marry thrice!

I chuckled.

"You, there…youngster!" I started back from the tomb, startled by the disembodied voice in the darkness. For a moment I thought one of the dead had come back to drag me in to his tomb! But it was the Red mask merchant. Cursing my own luck, I realized he'd placed his cart not far from the graves I had been reading.

"Come closer, I want to speak to you," he said.

"I think I'll spare myself your company," I said. "We are done with our trade. You should be happy, you had the upper hand."

"I have no wish to gloat. I was going to offer to share my fire with you," he said.

"I have my own fire to worry about," I replied, not caring how rude I sounded. "Besides, it is better to be alone than with a Red chrome. Especially one that trades in the masks of dead warriors!"

"That what you thought, was it?"

"That's what I saw!"

"The eyes often only see what the heart wishes them to," he said. "I do not trade bronze masks, especially those taken from dead warriors. I am bringing them to Ayas so that the Blues can return them to the Black nation. The Blues have always been good intermediaries between the Red chromes and the Blacks."

"I don't believe you!" I said, unwilling to give any Red the benefit of the doubt.

"Believe what you will," he replied. "Despite your arrogance and your ignorance, I still sense there may be some good in you." Even though his voice was calm, his words cut through me like a knife. This decaying Red chrome thought that he could dispense judgments to me! A Black chrome, superior to his kind in every way. How dare he! I moved closer to him. "The only chrome that could ever speak to me in that way was my father and he is dead – killed by you Reds!"

"Really?" he said. "I did not know Green Chromes were at war with us."

Realizing too late the mistake I made, I hastily replied, "Not all Greens are the same." Then I started to walk away.

"Wait!" He cried out. "I'm sorry if I offended you. And I'm also sorry for your loss. I too lost my father when I was young. I have lost a great many chromes that I cared for."

I turned around. I had no way of knowing if this was true or not, but he sounded sincere. And now, as I looked at him I thought I picked up an air or aura of worn weariness about him, as though he might well be someone who had no need to lie. I took a few steps closer to his fire. "Come, sit with me," he said, looking up. "Let us begin our conversation, again. Do not be afraid."

"I'm not afraid," I said. To prove it I hunkered

down near him.

He nodded.

"If you aren't a merchant of masks, why did you buy mine?" I asked him.

"Because you and your friend seemed desperate," he replied. His words were soft spoken, but I remained wary. He placed more wood in the fire. "I understand your anger. More than you can imagine."

"I'm not angry," I told him.

"Good," he replied, stoking the flames with a stick. "I have a question for you. I wonder whether you will answer it truthfully?"

Before I could say anything, he leaned in close and whispered, "what is a young Black chrome doing masked as a Green?"

8. Harvest Faire

"You are mistaken!" I said, with as much conviction as I could muster.

"Settle down my young friend, your secret is safe with me," said the Red chrome as he took something out of a sack and handed it to me. "Here, this is for you."

It was my mask; the black mask of celebration that Astor had sold him for three bronze coins. I hesitated. "Go on, take it. Now I know it belongs to you."

I took it from him and held it for a moment like the most precious of gifts. But then, as much as I wanted to keep it, I forced myself to return it.

"It was sold. It is mine no longer, but yours."

"If it is mine then I am free to do with it as I please. And I insist you take it. And don't let anyone ever make you part with it again."

I gingerly accepted the mask back again, running my fingers over its smooth curves.

"It was given to me by my father." I told him.

"I am certain he must have been a good chrome," he replied.

I nodded, fighting tears.

You lost your father and I lost my son in the war," he said, looking in to the fire. The reflection of the flames danced like spirits on his gray mask. "He was so young. His time came too early."

"The gods must think very highly of him to summon him so soon," I said.

He turned towards me and then, unexpectedly, took off his mask and placed it on the ground.

"It is night," he said. "And in the darkness, we are free to take these evil things off." He gave my arm a gentle squeeze. "Thank you for your kind words. I was right, your heart is noble. My instincts never betray me. I only wish I had the same faith in the gods that you have."

I studied his face, which glowed in the light of the fire. I had never seen the face of a Red chrome before. Maybe, because they had been our enemies, I was expecting that he would look different from us Blacks, but I was mistaken. He had long silver hair and deep lines on his forehead, no doubt carved by the passage of time and the toll of his loss. He was certainly older than my father had been.

"You can take off your mask too, if you wish," he said, settling himself down.

I was reluctant to do so and hesitated. But then I removed the small wooden mask Astor had made me. It wasn't mine anyway; it never fit my face well. To be free of it was actually a relief. We exchanged formal greetings and I learned that his name was Chtomio. As much as I wanted to hate him for being a Red chrome, I could not. For Chtomio's heart, like his words, were sincere and had no trace of hatred for either me or the Black nation, in spite of his son's death. He spoke slowly and softly, the way wise chromes do and I imagined he must have been an elder of some sort in the Red kingdom.

"I will ask no more questions about your Green disguise," he said, "but some words of advice from an old chrome; leave your companion as soon as you can and make sure whatever path you take does not entwine itself with his."

This took me by surprise. I did not know whether to say something, get up and walk away, or simply remain seated by his fire. I did not realize I had already chosen, for there I remained. "Astor is my friend," I said, nodding at the wooden mask, "he even made this for me."

"I have seen chromes like your friend many times on the Cancerian and on other roads," Chtomio replied. "Like scavengers, they hunt for food and for goods, and also like scavengers, they hunt at night, taking as theirs what is not theirs to take."

"But Astor isn't a scavenger!" I protested. "He is a good Green chrome who follows the teachings of the Mother Goddess."

"Assuming such a deity exists," continued Chtomio, "I doubt she would want to have anything to do with a chrome such as him. Too many times the gods are called upon to justify despicable actions carried out in their name."

These words deeply troubled me. Astor wasn't a thief! But then I remembered that he stole our horse from the farmer and I had been his willing accomplice. I blushed with shame. He had justified his actions with accomplished ease and I had believed him; his words had made perfect sense. But now Chtomio's words sounded like a verdict without appeal. Astor was a thief. In my heart, I knew it as well.

Chtomio then offered to share his dinner. I thanked him but refused, for I still needed to feed the horse as well as some time to think about what he had said. So I took my leave and when I returned to the tree where our horse was, I found Astor pacing in a circle around the animal. He was agitated. "Where have you been?" He demanded.

"Searching for firewood and hay," I answered, uncomfortably aware that I had returned empty handed, after spending so much supposedly looking for it. Astor pointed at me.

"What's that you're holding?"

"My mask. The Red chrome returned it to me."

He came closer to see it. He looked at it for a moment, thoughtful. Then he said: "Good. Forget about the fire and the horse, we have work to do. We need merchandise for the Faire."

"You want to steal from other merchants?" I asked, Chtomio's words still fresh in my ears.

"Shh!" Astor's eyes darted furtively around. "You and that mouth again! What did I tell you?" He placed both his hands on my shoulders, pressing down on them until it became uncomfortable. Lowering his voice further he said: "I told you that you need to adapt or you will not survive out here. Do you not believe me? You should. I have survived out here for more solstices than I can count. Certainly more than you."

There was no warmth or humor in his voice or in the steely glare of his eyes. I didn't doubt that if he thought it would profit him, he would betray me in an instant. Chtomio was right, all the evidence supported him. The chrome I thought had befriended me was, in reality, a coldhearted thief.

"Everyone will be asleep soon," he said. "Then we get to work. We move quietly and take one or two things from each cart. Not the fanciest things, mind you, but not the worst, either."

"I thought you followed the teachings of the Mother Goddess. But you're a common thief."

For a moment I was convinced I had let my tongue lead me in to trouble yet again. But Astor took a moment to cast me over a glance and then he nodded over at a few tents and carts resting nearby. "Do you think that any of those merchants make an honest trade? They rely on profiting from the ignorance of others. They buy low and sell high, they lie and they cheat and they convince poor, ignorant chromes that they are doing them a favor, that we should be thankful. Tell me, who is the real thief? Me, taking a morsel here and there so that I can live, or them, that take and take and take and keep on taking, even though they have much more than they will ever need?"

I had never thought about these things the way Astor did, not until he explained them to me. He saw the look of doubt on my face and continued: "You've seen how they treated us," he reminded me, "as if they were better than us Greens!" After the conversation with Chtomio, as much as I had sympathy for the Green, I could not in all honesty feel like I belonged to the chromes of the Mother Goddess. I was and always would be a Black chrome. And a Black chrome would never stoop so low.

I shook my head. "I cannot do it, Astor. I won't do it, no matter what you say."

"Then let me put it another way," he said while his eyes leveled at me "If you don't do it, I will tell everyone who you are and what you did in Axyum. Understood?"

"And just what is it he did in Axyum?" someone asked.

Chtomio emerged from the shadows.

"These are not matters that concern you, Red merchant," hissed Astor. If he was surprised, he surely didn't show it.

"Oh but they do," Chtomio replied. "When a young chrome is being forced into doing something he does not want to do, it is every older chrome's responsibility to prevent it. It is one of the Collective Laws as I am sure you recall."

Astor backed down and even broke in to something of a smile. "He's my friend. We were just talking amongst each other, weren't we, Asheva?"

I did not know what to say or do. Chtomio came closer. I noticed he carried a thick wooden staff.

"Friends, true friends, do not abuse their friendship with another to further their own ends," said

Chtomio. "They help us lead a life of rectitude by lending a hand in times of need, without expecting anything in return."

"Do you think I'm afraid of you, old merchant?" Astor snorted.

"I think that you are probably too arrogant and too stupid to be afraid of me. Leave the youngster be and continue your journey alone."

Astor took several steps towards Chtomio, ready to shove him on the ground, but the Red chrome shifted his body, just enough, to avoid the attack. As Astor lunged past him, he swung his staff at his legs, which still had not completely mended. Screaming with pain, Astor fell, landing hard.

"You'll pay for this!" he snarled at us. "Both of you!"

As I watched Astor on the ground, I saw that fires were beginning to be lit up again as the chromes in the caravans closest to us had heard the screams and were now coming out to see what was happening.

"Come," said Chtomio, putting his hand on my shoulder. "Leave him." We left Astor and made our way back to the Red Chrome's fireplace.

"You are free to do as you wish, Asheva, but I will be glad to have your company in Ayas."

"Don't you want to know what happened in Axyum before you travel with me?" I asked.

"Only if you wish for me to know. Otherwise, we will not speak of it further."

I nodded and thanked him, although I was still confused about what had happened. Part of me knew that I had done the right thing in leaving Astor, but another part felt like I had betrayed him. He had helped me after all, and now I'd turned on him. That night I did not sleep well, worried that Astor might try to take his revenge. When I did finally fall asleep I dreamt of demons and monsters that wanted to hang me. I tried to run from them, but the only place I could reach was a river. There, I was swept away by a wild current and though I struggled to find my way back to the bank, the water pulled me down slowly.

I awoke to the sun, hot and yellow against my eyelids, glad my nightmare was over. I crawled out from under Chtomio's cart where I'd slept on a blanket. The Cancerian already bustled with chromes and conveyances as they continued making their way towards Ayas.

Chtomio was busy putting his things back on the cart and preparing the horse. When he noticed that I had woken, he offered me honey and cheese. I slid under the cart again to eat it, so that no one could see me without mask in daylight. I was so hungry I crammed it all into my mouth in moments.

After, we hitched up his horse and moved away from the field, back onto the road. I scanned the crowd for Astor, but couldn't see him. When we passed by Sestertiu's pyramid tomb I saluted, telling Chtomio what I knew of him.

He nodded. "To Ayans, the tombs are sacred just like the Cancerian. This road is a vein for them, bringing life and nourishment. Without it, they would be dead."

"What do you mean?" I asked.

"The Cancerian passes all the territories before

it reaches the Blue plains. If anything happens along it, the lifeline to Ayas stops."

"I don't understand," I said confused

"The Blue thrive in commerce. It is the only thing they know how to do. Without it, Ayas would perish."

"But Astor told me they are very powerful."

Chtomio shook his head. "It is often those who have the least power who try to convince you they have the most," he said. "But don't be fooled, Asheva. To make sure that the Cancerian always remains as an open pathway, part of the Blues' wealth goes back to other territories."

As I listened to Chtomio's words I could not help but think of how knowledgeable other chromes were of the territories. In Axyum, no one spoke much of the other chromes and for the first time I began to wonder why that was.

The closer we got to Ayas, the more crowded the Cancerian became. In the distance, I could see something that resembled a glossy, indigo mountain; the famed Blue Pyramid of Ayas. So polished were the splendid blue sapphires crowning its peak, they radiated a soft azure light all around it. The towering stone walls of Ayas became visible too, stretching out to the left and right of us until they disappeared in the distance.

Ayas was enormous, at least compared to Axyum. I would not have been surprised if it was three or four times the size of my native city. By comparing some of the landmarks, I estimated that the pyramid must have been at least five times the height of the city's highest tower. I couldn't wait to pass through the gates and explore this marvelous place!

As if reading my mind, Chtomio said: "quite a sight isn't it? It never ceases to amaze me. And every time I come back here, Ayas gets bigger."

"How?" I asked. "It is confined by its walls."

"The Blue chromes simply build new outer walls around it. You'll see when we get there."

Every tower boasted huge flags of different colors that snapped smartly in the breeze. In amongst them was a black one. I glanced around to see if I could spot any Black chromes. Even though I was clothed in green, I was still worried they were after me. But I saw none. The Black were not known for their abilities in commerce anyway and the war against the Reds had made their presence at such fairs even less likely.

The city's entrance was a gilded archway more than fifty rods tall which marked the end of the road. Two magnificent blue banners were hung on each side of the arch. They were edged in brocade spun from real gold. Our horse stopped as we joined a queue of hundreds of chromes and their animals.

"Why the holdup?" I asked.

"The Blue require an excise fee to be paid at the entrance," sighed Chtomio. Several Blue guards were busy inspecting goods while others accompanied two dignitaries intent on collecting coins from all the visitors.

"I don't have any coins," I told my new friend.

"The fees are for carts. It's the goods they are after, not the chromes."

Behind the walls, a disjointed yet pleasant mix of music, perfumed scents, and the call of chromes hawking their wares could be heard. When we finally passed through the gates I was overwhelmed by the sheer spectacle of it all. It truly was an assault on all of the senses. The atmosphere was that of a great and never ending feast. I was dazzled by colors, many of which were new to me. Ayas' streets were awash with fire reds and saffron yellows, with lavender violets and indigo blues. There was green too, sparkling gem tones that ran from mint to jade. Pennants, silk ribbons, and precious stones decorated every available space.

Everywhere I turned, there were elaborate stalls. Many were far more luxuriant than my own humble house in Axyum. They resembled a bright confection of miniature palaces or jewel boxes. And the goods these merchants sold! Anything you could possibly want was here. Fine robes, spices, silks, masks, stones and healing powders I could recognize, but some of it was so strange I couldn't even begin to fathom its use.

My ears were assailed by a thrilling mix of foreign melodies, played on instruments I'd never seen before. My nostrils were filled with aromatic, pungent scents that ranged from sweet to musty to tangy. Truly, the Harvest Faire would be something I'd remember for the rest of my life.

"Chromes of all colors! Behold, the finest silks from Papylia!" cried one Violet chrome.

"Emotion potions – induce any type of feelings you desire, in yourself or others!" shouted another.

She wore a funny, two-toned mask, half red and half purple. Half of her painted mouth smiled while the other half cried.

"This way to the best sweet pork and nectar in the plains. Satiate yourselves, O hungry merchants!" chanted a short and chubby Yellow chrome surrounded by steam, from his stall. Perhaps because of the steam, the color of his mask was no longer yellow but of a strange pinkish color and I couldn't help but feel a resemblance between him and the pork he was proposing.

Amidst such raucous noise and boisterous activity, I was amazed that our cart continued to move, albeit very slowly. The inside of Ayas contained other walls, just like Chtomio had explained, showing how the city had extended in time. The result was one giant labyrinth where you could easily get lost if you did not know your way. Luckily for me, I had Chtomio.

The Blue Pyramid dominated the scene, standing in the middle of an enormous, circular open space. "The Ayans call this place Sfero Platia," said Chtomio. "The heart of the city." The open circus was surrounded by an array of beautiful buildings made of pink granites. They were all slightly curved to form a sweeping oval shape around the pyramid. I learned these were home to the most important barons of Ayas. But the most amazing sight lay below my feet. Instead of cobblestone, the entire grounds of the Sfero Platia were covered in mosaic tile. There must have been thousands upon thousands of intricate murals, all rendered in different shades of blue. They depicted various scenes, mostly of Blues doing what they did best, commerce.

Chtomio found a clean stable for his horse in the great Blue Pyramid's shadow. He locked up his cart and took out a single bronze mask. "I must find the dignitaries who have agreed to return these masks to the Black nation," he said. "Meanwhile, why don't you take a look around the faire? I'm sure you'll find something to interest you," he added cheerfully. "We'll meet back here at sunset, after the last ringing of the pyramid's bell." He pointed upward to a beautifully crafted bronze bell at the pyramid's crown. "The Blues use that to set out time vigils inside the faire. What do you say?"

Bursting with excitement, I happily agreed. The first place I visited, on Chtomio's recommendation, was inside the Blue Pyramid itself where he had promised I'd find the best stalls to be seen at the faire. I made my way in, where I saw imposing stalls neatly arranged in rows. The space was so large, I counted twenty rows. "Each row has different types of goods," Chtomio had told me before he left. "One is for clothiers, another for those who sell spices, yet another features arms."

"Which row is the best?" I had asked.

"The last row to the far right is certainly the most interesting," he said. "Those chromes hail from remote places and they have very bizarre goods to sell."

He had not exaggerated. There were things there I could have never imagined existed. Two female chromes from the Violets were using winged feathers to waft the scent of jasmine and rose around their stall.

One of them indicated a set of small, colored ampoules behind her. "These precious vials contain none other than the tears of Ardithya, the goddess of beauty," she cried. Many female chromes seemed to have been captured by this Violet's spell.

The stalls ranged from the sublime to the bizarre. One Blue chrome had a large group of curious on-lookers huddled around his stall. I couldn't even see the goods he was selling. All I could hear was his voice.

"Trample your neighbors if you wish to buy well today. You can always repent to your gods, tomorrow!" he said to cheers of laughter.

After a few moments, someone moved away and I was able to squeeze in and see what the fuss was all about. There, laid in front of me were a number of small glass spheres, each with what seemed like colored smoke inside.

The Blue chrome immediately zeroed in on me, much to his customers' amusement. "Look at this Green yokel ogle!" He said. "It's like he's never seen a vitra sphere before in his life!" When I confessed that indeed I had not, he gleefully told me the spheres were the product of the Red kingdom's finest glassmakers. "But it is only when they are brought here in Ayas that I place in them a special liquid made by the gods, to transform them from ordinary to extraordinary."

"How so?" I asked.

He lowered his voice. "These spheres not only reveal your true self, they predict your future."

I held one of the spheres up to my mask. But before I could look into it, the chrome swiftly snatched it back from me.

"Not so fast, youngster" he said, as everybody laughed. "You want to see your future, there are secret words to be said. You want to know which words, you have to buy the vitra."

"I don't have any coins with me right now." I had wished now more than ever that I had not lost the coins my mother had given me.

"Well then, no coins, no future," replied the chrome before turning back to the crowd "Come on, then! Who wants to buy one?"

I decided to go on to the next stall where one Orange chrome sold golden insects which moved as if they were real. "Can they fly too?" I asked astonished. "Yes, and talk as well!" snapped the chrome who had obviously overheard my conversation with his neighbor. "Go away, Green! You're making us weary with your presence." Up until then I did not fully grasp the weight of Astor's words about what it meant to be a Green at the faire, but I was learning quickly. I decided to shrug it off, as nothing would spoil my day at the market.

But something was about to. I had been so excited by all the stalls I had not noticed something that had been placed on a platform right in the middle of the pyramid. It was a sort of wheel, similar in type to those used to power mills. Something hung from it like a long sack of flour. As I went nearer, the wheel's real purpose became apparent; it was a torture machine of some kind. There was a mutilated body strapped inside it, attached to several steel spokes that radiated from the center of the grotesque wooden contraption all the way to its outer rim. The weight of the body had tilted the wheel in such a way that the spread-eagled corpse dripped blood on the floor. Other than being careful not to step in this ghoulish puddle and dirty their shoes, passing chromes were otherwise unconcerned by the tragic sight.

Horrified, I stopped one Yellow chrome and asked about the evil mechanism. "Must be your first time here," he said, glancing me over. "The Wheel of Chance is the reason why no one steals anything at the faire. Any chrome reckless enough to try," he added, nodding over his shoulder at it, "will find this waiting for him at the end of his adventure."

"Poor soul," I muttered.

"Save your sympathy," said the Yellow. "That thief hangs there as a reminder to everyone to keep their hands to themselves."

He explained that the Wheel of Chance was so named because it was chance that proved whether a chrome was guilty or innocent. A female chrome-at-arms, wearing a blind, eyeless mask in representation of the goddess of chance, threw ten knives at the accused while the wheel spun rapidly with the poor chrome strapped to its spokes. As far as this "tradition" went back in time, one could count on the fingers of a single hand how many had survived it. They were so hideously maimed, those who died were considered the lucky ones.

Now the Yellow took a closer look at the corpse. "This fellow's a Green. Maybe that's why you find it so upsetting," and with that, he hastened away.

For a moment, I thought the dead chrome

attached to the wheel was Astor. It made me sick, because I did not wish him any ill will. I moved closer and saw that the mask had been strapped on the victim's head so as not fall. Nevertheless, part of his face was visible from a corner and I was relieved in a grim way to see this unfortunate was not the trickster Green I'd traveled with.

In hindsight, I should have known better than to remain in this city after seeing such a gruesome example of barbaric Ayan justice. But we chromes are mere mortals, whose fate is also in the hands of chance. Never would that prove truer for me than in Ayas.

9. The Wheel Of Chance

I tilted my head and looked up at the distant, mirrored roof of the Blue Pyramid. It was supported by long wooden girders, studded with innumerable torches to provide light for the market. Then I gazed at each of the pyramid's four sides which featured its own, spacious entrance, cleverly angled to make the most of the sunlight and fresh air that flowed through. I was so pre-occupied with taking in the sheer size and scale of everything around me that I did not see a chrome cross my path. I stumbled into him and we both fell on the ground. Jingling coins scattered around him.

"I'm sorry," I said, getting up. Then, as I held out my hand to help him I recognized the wooden mask that belonged to Astor.

We stared at each other for an instant, without saying anything. I scooped up his coins, intending to hand them back to him. But just as I did, I saw the bloodstains on them. They were the same coins that had been tinged with the Eldest's blood during my last night in Axyum. I had not lost the coins my mother had given me after all. Astor had stolen them from me!

Before I could confront him, someone shouted: "Harlequin!" Fear gripped me. I instinctively looked around to see where the harlequin might be, but I only saw horrified chromes stopping what they were doing and standing rock still. They were all looking at me.

"Harlequin!"

Astor was pointing his finger straight at me.

"He's a Harlequin! I've seen him disguised as a Black chrome and a Green! But he's a Harlequin and he tried to steal my money!"

None of the chromes around us moved or said a word. They all seemed to be paralyzed by fear.

"I'm not a Harlequin!" I screamed at the top of my lungs. "He's lying. I'm not! He's the one who stole from me!"

"He is," insisted Astor. "And I can prove it! He has a black mask underneath his mantle! Check and see!"

Chromes pressed in around us. The Blue merchant of spheres elbowed his way to the front of the crowd, nodding at Astor. "What this young Green says is true," he said. "This youth induced erratic colors in one of my spheres when he held it." The crowd murmured their concern as the sly rogue then continued, "my vitra spheres are the best! The most accurate! And most reasonable for any who wish to purchase them."

"Get some ropes!" someone shouted.

"Call the guards!" cried another.

I was caught like a rat in a cage. If I didn't move now and quickly, I would be done for. I scanned around the circle of hostile chromes crowding in on me and identified two of the smallest and weakest looking ones standing next to one another. I ran at them, barging my way out between them.

"Quick, catch him before he gets away!" I heard Astor yell. And get away I did. I bolted to the nearest of the four exits as panicked chromes all around scrambled to avoid me.

"Don't touch him!" bellowed a Red. "Harlequins carry diseases!" Their outrageous lies fueled my anger, but they also cleared a path for me. All I had to do was make it outside and look for a quick way to escape from Ayas.

I had made it to within a rod or two of the pyramid entrance when a net fell over me. Stumbling, I kicked and punched several of the Blue guards who tied the cast net, with me still in it, to a pole. In no time at all I was trussed up like a game animal. Cheers of relief and joy went up all about me. Amidst the commotion, I could no longer see Astor. That liar scoundrel had given everyone the slip once more.

The guards lugged me out into the Sfero Platia as news that a Harlequin had been captured in Ayas sped ahead of them. A new crowd, twice as large as the one inside the pyramid, now gathered outside in the circus. I didn't stop struggling; doing all I could to make sure the guards had a difficult time carrying me through it.

I focused on numbing myself to all the insults and objects hurled at me. I kept thinking this was not happening; it was all just a bad dream. Soon, I'd wake up in my house in Axyum and get ready to go to the seminary. But now more guards appeared and unfortunately for me, they were very real. The crowd started chanting: "Kill him! Hang him!" Overcome with fear, I could not repel the image of the young harlequin I'd seen hanged in Axyum.

The guards wound their way through the crowd, showing me off like a prized trophy. They headed toward a palace, whose giant doors opened to receive us. As they did, I spotted a familiar Red chrome running close to the guards. My heart leapt – it was Chtomio! I yearned to tell him I wasn't a harlequin. Surely he couldn't believe the hissing, baying crowds could he? But I choked on my words. Chtomio didn't say anything. He just gave me a small nod. I was not sure if it was intended to comfort me or accuse me.

The palace doors clanged closed behind us, blessedly muffling the noise of the howling crowd outside. Whoever lived in here was obviously very important, for the entrance led to a courtyard full of statues and a lush garden. In the middle, a large marble fountain modeled after a goddess of some sort splashed water into several stone basins. She wore a crown full of blue sapphires and her supple arms held a basket full of wheat and fruits.

An imposing chrome stepped out from behind the fountain. He wore a fine blue mantle, a triangular headdress and an unusually large and elaborate shining, diamond-studded mask. As he drew closer, I saw his mask depicted two faces, each a different color. The white was made from crushed diamonds while the blue was fashioned from sapphires. Both glittered in the sunlight, blinding me.

All the guards stood at attention, as a sign of either respect or fear – most likely both. This chrome was clearly someone who held much power and wealth in Ayas; no doubt he was one of the barons Astor had mentioned. Thinking about Astor made my blood boil; he'd stolen my coins, accused me of the worst possible sin for a chrome and now left me to be killed. It angered me to think I might not live long enough to seek my revenge on him.

The guards released me from the net and spilled me on to the floor, where I stayed huddled and crouched as the double-faced baron circled me. "Do you know who I am, Harlequin?" he asked. His tone reminded me of the Eldest in Axyum, the arrogant voice of one used to authority and power.

"I do not, Your Highness. And I am not a Harlequin." I said.

This went ignored. "I am Staffan Viura," he said, "Grand Vizier of Ayas and baron of the gem trade. I am the eyes and ears of this city, master over its life and its death.

"Your highness, I am not a Harlequin!" I repeated, my voice laced with fear.

"Silence, you obscene creature! A Harlequin lies as readily as it breathes. I know one of your foul kind when I have the misfortune to look upon him. Tell me, how many more of you have infested our city?"

"I don't know your Highness, for I swear on all

the gods, I am not a Harlequin."

"Take him to my dungeon," Viura hissed to the guards. "He'll speak there."

As they hauled me to my feet, a voice called out from behind. "Wait! Your lordship, please!"

I looked around to see Chtomio, escorted by two Blue dignitaries, striding towards us. Surprised and affronted by the sudden and unannounced intrusion, the Grand Vizier addressed the two Blues with ill-concealed anger. "Why have you brought this Red chrome into my palace?"

One of the dignitaries approached the Grand Vizier and whispered something to him. He took a moment before turning to Chtomio. "So you are the dignitary sent by the Red kingdom to return the masks of the Black Army?" said Viura. "Does the Red kingdom now think itself so powerful it seeks to interfere with matters concerning our glorious city of Ayas?"

"Nothing could be farther from the truth, your lordship," said Chtomio as he knelt beside me and bowed his head. "I come not as a representative of my king, but as a humble wayfarer, who knows the youngster you have captured well, having met him on the Cancerian."

"So this Harlequin tried to deceive you, as well? Is that why you are here? You seek retribution?"

"No my lord, I came to speak for him. I do not think this young chrome is a Harlequin. But rather than probe in vain to determine his true nature, might I suggest we call on the goddess of chance to judge the matter?"

The Vizier seemed to contemplate the idea as he drummed his fingers on the masked chin. "Ah, I see. Let him take a ride on the Wheel of Chance? If he is guilty, the wheel will know."

"I am sure the wheel has divined many truths out of guilty chromes." Chtomio agreed.

"Speaking on behalf of the Goddess, I think she would be pleased by your suggestion," The Grand Vizier said.

I could not believe what Chtomio had just done. I shot him a look which must have made clear my sense of bitter contempt for him, because he couldn't hold my eye. He was sending me straight to the cruelest of deaths! I had been betrayed twice in one day by chromes I had counted on as friends. In that moment I wished more than anything that I had stayed to take my chances in Axyum. Better to die by the hand of my own kind than these treacherous rats.

"We shall stage a huge feast outside the Blue Pyramid!" declared the Grand Vizier, now quite excited by the prospect. "Chromes from every territory will see how Ayas treats Harlequins!" He glanced at me. "What a splendid entertainment he'll make at the Harvest Faire." Then he clapped his hands. "Tomorrow, when the sun is highest in the sky, the prisoner shall be judged by the Wheel of Chance. Let it be known throughout the city. So I have spoken, so it is ordered. Now take him away!"

"Your Highness, I beg you for mercy!" I cried out, but he had already turned his back on me to confer with Chtomio. I could hear the crowd outside the palace cheer the news of my impending trial.

Consumed by bloodlust, they were eager to witness the death of a fellow chrome, however guilty or innocent he may be, just as my own nation had been the morning my father had taken me to the execution. The roar reached a terrifying crescendo as I was brought out from the Grand Vizier's palace under heavy guard.

The city's Blue herald mounted a dais to issue a proclamation. His robes were bisected in blue and white and he wore an ice blue mask with a silver colored nose that looked like the beak of a rapacious bird. Addressing the throng in a shrill voice, he gestured broadly at me. If I hadn't been in so much trouble I might have found his theatrical moves comical. "This creature has been recognized to be a Harlequin!" He declared. A great roar, a cacophonous wail of hatred went up at mention of the word. The herald gave it time to rise, before raising his arms for quiet, drawing every bit of drama out of the moment. "However, the Grand Vizier, in his munificence, has decided to let the Wheel of Chance determine the fate of the accused."

Now the herald was interrupted by gleeful chants of: "The wheel! The wheel!"

Once again he allowed the outburst to continue for a moment before continuing. "Therefore, by order of His Grace, the wheel shall be placed in the Sfero Platia by mid-sun's vigil tomorrow. As usual, all chromes who attend shall pay no less than two bronze coins. Infants need only be counted with one coin of admittance."

The Palace guards loaded me into a cart which bore me through narrow streets and away from the open circus. Many of the crowd followed us in a macabre procession until we reached the base of a tower. There, I was handed over to more guards, who took me into custody. They dragged me down a spiral stairway that curled beneath the ground, deep in to the bowels of the earth. At the bottom of the stairs, they threw me inside a cell and locked the iron door.

I looked around. I was trapped in a cold, dark stone grotto with rotten straw on the ground to serve as my bed. Two guards remained stationed outside my door to guard me while the others trooped back up the stairs. Utterly bereft, I prayed to the gods of the Black nation.

One of my jailors thumped his ax against my door. "Save your prayers, Harlequin," he mocked. "Not even the gods can save you now!"

"If I were a Harlequin, don't you think I'd use my powers to fly out of this pigsty and stick you inside it?" I snapped.

"Don't talk to him," the other guard warned. "Harlequins like to play tricks on us chromes. Best leave him, lest he poisons your mind."

"I ain't afraid of him," growled his companion. "Seen four Harlequins die, in my time. This one'll be my fifth."

He slowly removed his mask and grinned a wide, rotten-toothed smile. "Come this vigil, tomorrow, the vultures'll be gorgin' on his bones." And then the two of them started to cackle. A terrible, shrill noise that echoed about the cold stone walls.

I closed my eyes to try and distract myself from my misery. I thought of happy days spent with my father in Axyum. I tried to imagine what I would have become, had my destiny been different and our elders had made peace instead of war with the Reds. By now, I would have been in the Sacred Forest, together with my friends, concentrating on the Rite of Initiation. I would have become a devout son of the Black nation and followed in my father's footsteps.

My thoughts turned to the Eldest of Axyum. Would he have tried to hurt us if my father had been alive? Were the other elders worthy of the Black nation and of our peoples' devotion? How had they become elders anyway, given that the Eldest was not even as old as my father? Ironically, the more I thought about these things, the harder it was for me to keep the reality of my present situation at bay. A harsh, burning feeling of injustice coursed through my body. Why wasn't anyone fighting for the right things? If my father and his fellow warriors knew what I knew about the elders, surely they would have returned home and fought against them instead of the Reds. It tore at me that it was now too late for me to do anything about it all.

My anger directed itself at others, too. Why hadn't Chtomio fought to save his son from the war? How come Astor didn't use his wit and skills to be anything but a thief?

"Why am I going to die for something I am not?" I uttered out loud, unable to hide from it any longer.

I was going to die come next sunrise; by all rights I should have been terrified. But instead I felt outraged for not having been given the chance to battle the wrongs that swirled around me. I paced nervously up and down my cell, no longer bothering to pray to the gods for mercy. On the contrary, I was angry at them, too. They were the most selfish of all! They had not given me enough time to fulfill my destiny so I could make things right. They were to blame for all the misery in the territories. What did they do to aid the righteous? Nothing!

I don't know when I fell asleep but when I woke, two new guards had replaced the previous ones, indicating that much time had passed. I asked them for food and water, but they ignored me. My thirst was intolerable, so when another group of guards came down the stairs rattling with a chain, I was glad the time to put an end to my agony had arrived. To my surprise, these guards offered me fresh clothes.

In the darkness of the dungeon I could not see what kind of a cloak they forced me to wear. When they deemed me ready, they clamped the chain on me, and lead me like a dog up the stairs. But before they did that, they removed my wooden mask I had placed on.

"Harlequins don't wear masks!" snapped one of the guards.

"Give it back to me!" I said. The thought of not having a mask in front of the crowd was something unbearable. In my whole life, I had never been in public without a mask.

They laughed. I forced myself not to cry. I wouldn't give these animals the satisfaction. Outside the tower, the sun blinded me. "Please," I said to them again. "Give me a mask. Any mask!"

Ignoring me, they hoisted me onto a cart with a pole mounted on top. As they tied me to it, I looked down. The tunic they had given me was fashioned from different colored patches. Just like a real Harlequin, I thought. The travesty was complete.

The cart lurched forward. Moments later, as we approached the Sfero Platia I could hear the deafening roar of the crowd, more powerful than a thousand peals of thunder. Then we clattered our way into it. There were chromes everywhere I looked; below me, above me, clinging to the pyramid, leering out of windows. They shouted insults and hurled their scorn upon me like rotting fruit. My first reaction was to close my eyes, but then surprising even myself, I reopened them and gazed about. Incredibly I still felt no fear, only contempt. Perhaps because part of me felt I was already dead.

My cart continued its slow journey towards the center of the square. Following the Great Vizier's order, his lackeys had moved the Wheel of Chance outside so that the maximum number of chromes could witness my sentence. It looked bigger to me than before, which wasn't surprising. Cleaned, polished, and emptied of its previous occupant, it awaited a new guest.

A large stage had been erected in front of the Blue Pyramid. The Grand Vizier stood upon it, acknowledging the cheering crowd. A phalanx of other Blue dignitaries, as well as chromes from other territories, stood with him, basking in the applause. One among their number edged forward: A Black chrome! Instinctively, I wanted to call for help but fought the urge. It would have meant going from the wheel to the gallows.

When the cart finally stopped in front of the Wheel of Chance, the crowd fell silent. I was led down from the cart, amongst a circle of guards. I spotted Chtomio standing just behind them.

"Have faith in the gods!" he shouted at me.

The guards dragged me up onto the wheel's platform before I could reply.

"Kill him!" I heard a group of chromes scream.

"Torture the Harlequin!" cried a female chrome. "Rip his guts out!" hollered her daughter, before being shushed by the mother with a clip around the ear. The guards strapped me by the waist onto the wheel's main spokes. Then they bound my arms and legs with tight ropes to the back of it. Two guards below me held the wheel still, keeping me in an upright position, facing straight ahead to another platform that would be used by the blind, knife-wielding chrome-at-arms. When this was done, several horns sounded.

"Blue chromes, fellow merchants!" the Vizier exclaimed. "As our Harvest Faire draws to a close, what better way to end it than by witnessing the spectacular and just Wheel of Chance in action?"

Chromes enthusiastically nodded and applauded their approval.

"Today, it is up to the gods to decide whether or not the rogue strapped to our wheel, is a Harlequin!"

"He's a Harlequin, all right!" A fat, Blue chrome merchant crowed. "I just bet a half sack of coins on it!"

"Die Harlequin!" an old hag in a dirty Green mask yelled.

"Normally," the Vizier continued, "the Goddess of Chance uses ten knives, but that is for common thieves. For a Harlequin, ten knives are not enough!"

The crowd roared like thunder once more.

"For this trial, no less than twenty knives shall suffice! And now, welcome the Goddess of Chance!"

On cue, in time to the chanting audience, a female chrome dressed in golden armor and a blue cloak was led onto the platform opposite mine by a guard. She was beautiful of form and wore an intricate mask of solid gold that covered her face only up to the mouth. Her guard turned her to face me. I struggled to see from this distance whether her eyes were really covered or not. Unfortunately, the sunlight reflected off her armor blinded me so I couldn't tell.

By her side was a small, ornate table. Even from this distance I could make out the long, sharp knives resting upon it. My executioner remained silent, concentrating. Then she inclined her head and made a sweeping gesture with her hand, the signal to start spinning the wheel. The guards below me worked a crank and I started turning. Within moments I was spinning fast in all directions; around, backwards, forwards, up and down. I felt dizzy and incredibly sick and dearly wished I had been given enough food so I could spew it out over the crowd. The sun's heat, combined with the motion made my head explode with pain. I was resigned to what was going to happen. Just let my end be swift, I prayed.

The female chrome took a deep breath and raised her arm. I closed my eyes. I heard the whooshing sound of the blade flying through the air. Against every instinct I forced my eyes open again, in time to see it arrowing right for me. Then a very strange thing happened. As I braced to feel it plunge in to my skin and sink deep in to me, it deviated away from my face to hit the wood rim of the wheel.

"Ohh," the crowd uttered in unison, disappointed. The guards slowed the wheel. My head continued to pound and my intestines felt liked they'd dropped down inside my throat. The golden-armored chrome got ready to hurl her second knife. This throw was just as precise as her first and the blade flew true to its target. But it too flipped away from me at the last moment, grazing the hair of my left arm as it hit the rim and clattered away to the ground. The wheel was slowed even more, but the third and fourth knives veered away from me and missed, just like the first two. The fifth actually hit someone, but it wasn't me. It flew in to the neck of a chrome standing behind the wheel. His screams were loud and terrible enough to be heard throughout the circus and made the chromes nearer to the wheel pull back to a safer distance, creating further havoc amongst the spectators.

"He's performing magic! The Harlequin is performing his magic!" the Vizier gasped. Undaunted, the Goddess of Chance continued to throw. Changing tactic, she threw her next set of knives at a quicker pace, one after the other. Six flew at me on a true course, each swerving at the last moment to miss me.

The mood below me began to shift. I could hear chromes begin to ask each other if what they were witnessing could be the sign of my innocence?

Hope began to creep up inside me. Maybe I would make it out of this alive after all? Again, the Goddess of Chance altered her style of throw. Now she took her time between throws. Her skill and aim were impeccable, yet her work was in vain. Nineteen knives had been thrown – and I remained miraculously unscathed.

Now, on a word from The Goddess, the wheel ground to a total halt. I saw the Vizier and his cronies and most in the crowd reduced to drop-jawed silence. Behind her mask, I sensed their Goddess of Chance was also doubting herself.

She carefully lined up her last knife at me, her blind face searching for her target as if she could zero in on my location by smell alone. She faked one throw and then another. On her third try, I watched in horror as the long sharp blade arced through the air, headed directly at my heart. I closed my eyes and heard a scream. For a moment I thought I'd been hit. How odd that I felt nothing. Maybe death was not as painful as all that after all?

I opened my eyes in time to see a guard below me stagger over to the stairs of my platform. As he turned I saw the final knife was embedded deep in his back. No one seemed to know what to do next. The entire square of chromes was locked in silence. While the guards helped their wounded companion, the Goddess of Chance instinctively turned toward the Grand Vizier for new instructions. Maybe she wasn't blind after all.

"The gods have spoken!" shouted someone, the voice echoing out across the dumbfounded crowd.

"Yes, we have all witnessed it!" came a familiar voice. "The gods have spoken and this is their verdict," Chtomio continued as he bounded up the stairs to my side. "You have all seen for yourselves. This young chrome is not a Harlequin!" he said, pointing to me. "And how could he ever have been? He's just a youngster!"

Seeing was believing. As I watched, most of the chromes began to nod their heads in approval. "Shame on us for having deprived him of his freedom. See how strenuously he was defended by the gods, as compensation for our woeful actions?" Chtomio concluded before turning to face the Grand Vizier.

"O Great Vizier! This humble chrome asks that your word be respected. Let your guards free this innocent at once."

"Free him! It's an omen!" I heard someone say. "Don't let the wrath of the gods upon us! Free him!"

I did not hear the Vizier's response to Chtomio's words, but judging from the promptness with which the guards came up to the wheel and freed me, he must have given his consent without much hesitation. Once the guards took the last rope from me, I fell on the floor. I felt someone lift me to my feet. It was Chtomio. "Do not faint, Asheva," he whispered. "We are not safe yet."

What happened afterward, how we got out of there and on to Chtomio's cart and away from the city I do not recall. What I do remember is lying comfortably in the back of the cart, watching the Blue Pyramid of Ayas slowly drift away from view. I was on the Cancerian again.

"Was it the gods that helped me? Or was it you?" I heard myself croak, still weak and groggy from my ordeal. Chtomio didn't answer at once. He took a moment before glancing down at me.

"Sometimes even the gods need a hand from us mortals," he replied.

"How did you do it?" I asked. "How did you make the knives steer away from me?"

He dug into a pocket of his red cloak and took out some dark, flecked rocks, showing them to me. "With these," he said. "There's a reason why the Goddess of Chance usually never misses. These rocks have a peculiar property. They attract certain metals, like the iron spokes of the Wheel." He told me that the Blues rubbed their blades with these rocks, so that the chrome-at-arms' knives would always find their victim.

"Then why wasn't I killed?"

Chtomio smiled. "If these same rocks are rubbed on the spokes, their power is inverted. Instead of attracting the knives, the wheel repels them."

"Magic!" I murmured.

"No, there is no magic involved, Asheva." he laughed. "There are so many things you still need to learn about the ways of the territories."

Chtomio went on to tell me that the previous night he had managed to sabotage the metallic spokes of the wheel with his stones, for the Ayans had left it unattended. "In any event I am forever grateful to you," I said.

"Don't be," he replied.

I closed my eyes and a tiredness I had never known swept over me. Even though I had been saved by Chtomio, I still felt like the gods had guided his hand and given me a second chance. The feelings I experienced with such intensity in the dungeon remained fresh in my mind: I was not going to let anyone take advantage of me anymore. I would no longer cower from injustice; I would seek it out and fight it in whatever territory I found it lurking, for I was certain this was the destiny the gods had intended for me to fulfill. It was why they had delivered me.

Then, another thought bubbled upward into my consciousness. I opened my eyes, again, and turned towards Chtomio. "You were the only one that believed I was innocent. If you know so many things, how do you know I'm not a harlequin?" I asked him.

"Because I am one," he said.

10. Revelations

I inhaled deeply, savoring the crisp, fresh air. It had a different scent to the plains, or even the lush, green hills surrounding Axyum. It tickled my nostrils until it felt like the very breath of life itself sweeping through me and reaching deep down into my soul.

I tried to get up, but my body wouldn't move. I could hear the wind blowing and the sound of thunder in the distance. No, it wasn't thunder. It was something else.

"Asheva," A voice quietly spoke my name.

Who was that calling me?

"Asheva, wake up."

I opened my eyes, but the light was too much, so I shut them tight again. I reopened them, this time squinting. At first everything seemed covered cast in orange, but then it began to turn blue. Everything was blue; it was overwhelming. I was facing the sea. The rolling thunder I heard were waves crashing onto the beach.

I had never seen such a large body of water before. I could do nothing but stare at it for a moment. My hands dug into the soft, whispering sand with a will of their own. It was cool and humid. I was in shadow too, under the shade of a pine tree. My arms and legs tingled. Then they began to ache.

"Where am I?" I asked. My mouth felt full of cotton.

"You're finally back from the dead," I heard a familiar voice say. "More precisely, between Red and Violet territory." I turned towards it and saw Chtomio's grey and white mask. The sight of it sparked horrifying images in my confused mind: the Wheel of Chance, the escape, the Harlequin.

Harlequin. Chtomio was a Harlequin! What had he done to me?

I tried to get up but the pain in my limbs was overwhelming. "Stay away from me, Harlequin!" I cried.

Chtomio took off his mask and smiled at me. "You were exhausted. You slept through our entire journey here."

My body shook, revolted by the thought of having been captured by a Harlequin. "Go away!" I bellowed at him. Chtomio widened his arms and spoke in his soothing voice: "If I wanted to harm you, I would have had done so already."

"Liar!" I spat. "I've heard all about the twisted things you do with chromes!

"Oh yes? Like what, for instance?"

"You take their blood and play with their remains." I backed away from him, but with the sea at my back there was nowhere to go. Then I spotted his weathered cart, a short distance away to my right. With every last bit of energy I had, I got up and stumbled towards it, fighting my pain and hoping the Harlequin would not seize me like a hawk snapping up its quarry.

Chtomio sat where he was as I reached the cart and mounted it, only to discover that the horse was not hitched to it. The beast stood placidly munching grass under another tree.

Now Chtomio got up. He went to the horse, untied it and led it toward the cart. "The Cancerian is a three day journey from here," he said. "On it, you can still find chromes like Astor who tried to deceive you; like the Blue Vizier who wanted to kill you or, I suppose, your own kind from whom you ran away. I wish you luck."

I glared at him, unsure of what to do. Pins and needles shot through my arms and legs. "What will happen to me if I stay here?" I asked.

"That depends on you," replied Chtomio.

"How so?" I asked.

He walked passed me and lifted a sack out of his cart. He opened it and removed a small silver barrel, half the length of my arm, holding it up for me to see. I stared at it, dumbfounded.

"Do you know what this is?"

I nodded. "It's a scopium," I said, still surprised to see such a precious instrument in the hands of someone that wasn't an Elder.

"Quite so. I'm sure the Black chrome elders use a similar one in Axyum," he said.

"They use it to verify a Chrome's color," I said.

"What do you say we verify your aura, to see if you really are a Black?" he said.

"Of course I am a Black!"

"In that case there's nothing to worry about, is there?"

He pointed the instrument at me and the little machine whirred into life, powered by I knew not what source. Chtomio put it to his eye and stared through it at me. "Hmm," he said.

What did "hmm" mean?

He offered the scopium to me. "Here, look."

I was afraid to touch it.

"Go on!" he said, "It won't bite you."

My hands were shaking.

"Point it at your legs."

I hesitantly reached out and took the instrument from him and looked through the barrel. Even though my leggings were dark and caked in mud and dirt, they began to turn red; deeper and deeper until they were the color of blood. I took the scopium from my eye, rearing back from it.

"So, what did you see?" asked Chtomio.

"I saw black," I lied. "What else would I have seen? Everything was black."

"Really?" said Chtomio, gently mocking me. "Are you sure it wasn't red?" He pointed the instrument at me again. "Ah no, sorry. My mistake. Your chrome is orange."

I grabbed the scopium back from him and looked through it again. Sure enough, my clothes and my flesh had now all turned into the color of the Orange chromes.

"This just proves that you are a Harlequin!" I said. "It's sorcery."

"No, Asheva," he said. "It proves that chromatic aura is a lie, just like all the other lies you have been told."

As he spoke, words I'd heard time and time again in Axyum came back to haunt me. Harlequins are liars; their intention is always to deceive and confuse – before they kill us.

"You're not a pure chrome," he said. "No one is. That kind of chrome does not exist."

"More lies!"

"We don't have any Chromatic color inside us. They simply don't exist."

"Blasphemy!" I cried. "I am a Black chrome, as my father was and his father before him. And all my ancestors -- to whom our land was handed down to by the Supreme God himself, Lapis, creator of the Black Nation!"

"No, Asheva. All a myth, spread during more primitive ages to unite hordes of feuding warriors and bring peace and order to our lands." Chtomio insisted.

"How far are you willing to go with your lies?" I hollered at him, disgusted. "And why? What good do they do you? I'll never believe any of them."

But Chtomio was not in the least bit disturbed by my contempt and he continued his story.

"Once united, however, those warriors began to quarrel again. They just could not resist the lure of greater power. This time, they formed clans, each one with a different color. Then, along came the so-called chromatic elders, sages and high priests who happily sold out for wealth and power by spreading the lies. They realized that uniting a clan under a color or a flag was not enough to preserve their power, so they came up with the myth of the chrome: an aura inside of you that was so strong that you could never part with it or mix it with another's."

I listened dumbfounded. Chtomio spoke blithely, unperturbed by the unnerving effect his words had on my young psyche, as if he were discussing wheat in the fields or the height of the sun in the sky rather than the fundamental truths of life. "The leaders of every clan, of every color used this despicable fabrication to demand loyalty and reinforce their power. They repeated it over and over, until doubt and fear pervaded every heart and the lie became truth. In time, the clans turned on one another and rejected peace and harmony and understanding in favor of war. Every clan went their own way, raising walls to defend their leaders' privileges, building new fortresses and cities, and making certain through so-called sacred rites that their lies were embedded deeper and deeper in the hearts and minds of each new-"

"Stop!" I cried, unable to listen to any more of it. I moved towards Chtomio, until my face was up close to his. "I'm a Black Chrome, son of the Black nation! Understand? I'm a son of the Black nation!"

I don't know how many times I repeated those words until everything I had heard overwhelmed me. "I want to go home to Axyum," I finally said, weeping like a lost infant and feeling even more shame because of it.

Chtomio sat down beside me. He spoke softly. "Then go. No one is holding you here. You are free to do whatever you choose."

I shook my head. "I can never go back."

With nothing more to lose, I told him why I had run away from home. I told him about the Eldest and how he had come to see my mother shortly after my father died in battle. I explained how he tried to have his way with her by threatening her with his position and power and when this didn't work, how he attacked her. I finished by telling him how I had killed the Eldest.

Chtomio listened, but I could see his eyes had become distant, as if he were thinking about other matters of more concern to him. "So you have killed the Black nation's Eldest," he said, his eyes narrowing. "I'm sure the elders did not mourn him too long." This time, there was no sarcasm in his tone.

"What do you mean?" I asked.

He stared at me straight in the eyes. "How many times had you seen your Eldest's face, unmasked, before he came to your dwelling?"

"Never," I replied.

"Precisely. The masks enable those in power to change leaders without anyone else knowing about it."

Chtomio was right. When he came to our house, it was the first time that I had actually seen the Eldest without a mask and I had been surprised that he was no older than my father, maybe even younger. So how could he have been the Eldest? And how had he become the Eldest in the first place if he was not amongst the wisest or most venerable of our nation?

As if reading my thoughts, Chtomio said "Now do you begin to understand how many lies they have told you, Asheva?"

"If these are all lies, how is it that no one knows the truth but you?" I asked, even more confused.

"I never said I was the only one," he replied. "Other chromes know what the truth is, the ones who hold power certainly do. But they would lose that power if the rest of the population were ever to know. Imagine, for a moment, that the Blacks and the Reds, or the Blue for that matter, realized that there is absolutely no difference between them. That, in fact, they are all the same -- and that their leaders had always known this. The leaders would have rebellion on their hands."

"Who are these chromes?"

"I told you who they are. They call themselves elders, or barons, or sages, or even kings. Each color has its lot. And as intent as they are in reinforcing the differences between chromes, the fact is they are as one when it comes to preserving their power, in more treacherous ways than you can possibly imagine."

Chtomio stood and dusted off his robe. "And yet, no matter what tricks they pull, there will always be someone who dissents. Ever since the clans divided, a courageous few have sworn never to forget the true history of our ancestors. They passed on what they knew to others that were willing to listen. They, in turn, passed it on to more chromes. Occasionally, some of them tried to fight the lies that had been planted so deeply in the roots of our souls. Those brave folks refused to wear masks and accept a color. So the elders and sages of each clan added yet another chapter to their farce. They began to vilify those brave souls who knew the truth, declaring they were no longer chromes. Instead, they were denounced as…"

"Harlequins," I whispered.

Chtomio nodded. "Harlequins."

"So Harlequins are just like… chromes?"

"My dear Asheva, Harlequins are chromes," he told me.

"And they have no magical powers?"

"Of course not."

"But I saw magic with my own eyes. The Harlequin we hanged in Axyum had an aura that left his body. It dispersed into the heavens with the colors of a rainbow. I saw it, Chtomio! It was real!"

"What you saw was probably colored powder blown from beneath the gallows. Over time, the keepers of this lie have become quite good at their tricks."

I tried to concentrate and think back to the abominable hanging scene in Axyum. I could still see the young Harlequin's scared face in front of me, but instead of the roaring crowd, there were now other sounds buzzing in my ears. They were the words that Chtomio used: tricks, masks, Harlequins, chromes; Harlequins *are* chromes. My head started going dizzy again. Harlequins are chromes. Chromes are Harlequins. Tricks and lies. The aura doesn't exist. I suddenly realized that my hands were trembling. But if all this was the case, then…

"Why doesn't the truth come out?" I asked.

"Because the truth is often harder to accept than a lie, and sometimes chromes prefer lies," Chtomio replied. "Truth must be given in small doses. Too much too soon can destroy a cause. That's why I need your help."

"To do what?" I said, still shocked.

"To unite the territories," he answered.

Don't miss the second, third and fourth books of The Red Harlequin Series, already on sale at Amazon!

Book 2 Kingdom Of Deceit

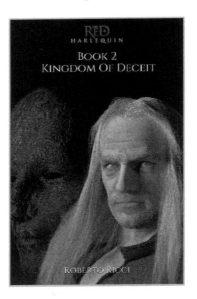

More deceit awaits Asheva, as he makes his way into Samaris. In the city of the Red Kingdom, his convictions about the Red clash with the reality of a land divided in castes. There, the Janis, members of the lowest caste, are left to live in abominable conditions. But turmoil is building, both inside the walls and outside where a violent attack takes the Reds by surprise...

Book 3 Rise Of The Harlequin

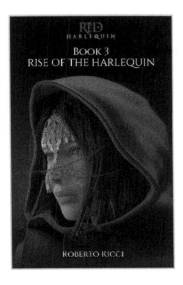

In Book Three, violence sweeps the territories as the Black Nation continues to bite at Asheva's heels, along with Cestia, the fallen Red Princess. Cestia has to rise above her own personal tragedy to uncover the truth about the chromes, the Harlequins and Asheva. Asheva, in the mean time, caught between the wrath of revenge and the desire for love, needs to fight his own demons.

Together, Cestia and Asheva vow to rise and fight the darkness that has taken hold of their world. And they do this first in the Twin Cities, where the Orange and Yellow chromes live and where divisions are not only based on the color of the chrome...

Book 4 A New Dawn

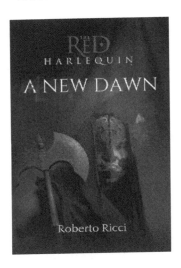

In Book Four, the war to end all wars has begun. Chromes of different colors need to unite and overcome their differences. In the mean time, the love between Asheva and Cestia is put to the test and the outcome is anything but certain...

Life, death, friendship, freedom...they all merge into a new, breathtaking journey into the territories, where a new dawn has just begun.

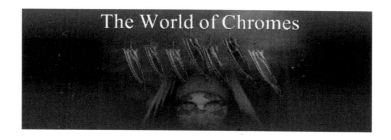

The World of Chromes

Enter a world where the only thing that matters is your color. A world divided into seven territories, each with its own characteristics:

1. THE BLACK CHROMES

The Black Chromes live in the city of Axyum and are warriors who are convinced they are superior to all other Chromes. Fearful of their gods, they believe that worldly conduct is an offense to them so they lead rigid, puritanical lives. According to legend, the Black Nation was created by the Shepherd God, who gifted the first Eldest with the Eastern Forests. These Forests remain a sacred place for the Blacks where they conduct important rites. Their historical enemies are the Red whom they see as the only other Territory that can compete for the supremacy of the lands.

Black Virtue: **Fortitude**
Black Sin: **Wrath**
Black Symbol: **Onyx**

The Black City of Axyum

2. THE BLUE CHROMES

The Blue Chromes are the most astute and successful merchants of all the Territories. The Chromes' most important fairs are held in the Blue city of Ayas, the biggest city of all the Territories. Such events have made the Blue the wealthiest Chromes of all. Such is their obsession for wealth that it is said that they leave their wars to be fought by other Chromes, for they only have time for their trade.

Blue Virtue: **Diligence**
Blue Sin: **Excess**
Blue Symbol: **Sapphire**

The Blue City of Ayas

3. THE RED CHROMES

Red Chromes are the "Athenians" of the Territories, intellectual and slightly haughty. They are divided into three castes: the Noble Ashis; the Sayis, who are tradesmen and soldiers; and the Janis, who are the untouchable. Only the Ashis and Sayis are allowed to live in the Red City of Samaris. The Janis on the other hand live in slums beyond the city's protective walls. According to legend, the twin Gods, Adio of the Sea and Adia of the Land, created the Reds. The Red Chromes control a lucrative salt trade, thanks of their close proximity to the sea.

Red Virtue: **Knowledge**
Red Sin: **Pride**
Red Symbol: **Ruby**

The Red City of Samaris

4. THE GREEN CHROMES

Green Chromes are nomadic, having lost their own Territory eons ago or at least that is what other Chromes say. They worship the Mother Goddess, mother of all creatures in nature, and are very cavalier about the way they've chosen to live. They are viewed as a poor sort of vagabond Nation and looked down upon by the other Chromes, but they believe themselves to be the luckiest Nation because they believe they have achieved harmony with all that surrounds them and can survive quite nicely off the bounty Mother Nature provides. Their most important rite is the Moksia, or the ability to camouflage with their surrounding so as to become one with the Mother Goddess. Other abilities include their storytelling, making music and performing.

Green Virtue: **Charity**
Green Sin: **Sloth**
Green Symbols: **Sunflowers and Serpents**

The Green City of Everdia

5 & 6 THE ORANGE & YELLOW CHROMES

Both these Mountain Nations live in adjacent territories where they do everything jointly (alliances, trade, etc.) They boast two twin cities and are politically malleable. Their only hard and fast rule is to ally
themselves with the dominant Nation and then use their position to try and take advantage of any unstable Nations. Besides extracting the gold from their mountains, they are also able farmers and cattle raisers, and mainly trade their meats with the Reds and the Blues. There is however one important peculiarity which distinguishes them from the other Chrome Nations...the Yellow are all male Chromes and the Orange are all female Chromes.

Yellow Virtue: **Humility**
Yellow Sin: **Greed**
Yellow Symbol: **Gold**

Orange Virtue: **Patience**
Orange Sin: **Envy**
Orange Symbol: **Orange Feather**

Doryca and Crodya, respectively the Yellow and Orange Cities

7. THE VIOLET CHROMES

The Violets are obsessed with beauty in all its forms. They are known for their esoteric perfumes and serums which they extract from the flowers in their land and which they trade with the other Chromes. They are travellers as they go through the Territories with their houses on wheels so they can both travel and take their comforts with them. They live in the Violet city of Papylia, known for the massive gathering of giant butterflies. They are a great source of news and gossip, as well.

Violet Virtue: **Kindness**
Violet Sin: **Narcissism**
Violet Symbol: **Lavender**

About the author

Roberto Ricci is a fiction writer of short stories, novels and screenplays. He has been amongst other things a journalist, an officer in the Italian Army and a Senior Executive in a children's entertainment company. He has attended NYU and the European Business School and has lived in Tokyo, New York, Rome, Milan, Paris and London.

www.amazon.com/author/robertoricci

The following eBooks are also available on Amazon from the same author:

2016: Stories From The Near Future

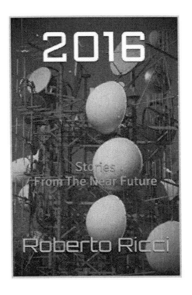

A collection of short stories from the not too distant future.

What if social networks suddenly turned from inclusive to exclusive? Where is all the huge amount of data that we produce daily going to be stored? Will we become virtually eternal? All this and more in 2016! A humorous (and slightly dark) view of the year ahead!

Parablu
Level 10
Sweet Dreams Inc.

In the year 2016…

…Anamast, a leading Search Engine Corporation, will sponsor an innovative virtual school program for children of all ages. But alas, innovation does not come without minor collateral damages. Fortunately Anamast will have a solution for that too: a blue liquid called *Parablu.*

…All social networks will merge into one and become known as Society. Society will stop being inclusive and start being exclusive. Users will be associated with a Level to define their personal and professional status. Changing one's profile will become almost impossible unless you are able to take part in the nation's favorite game show: *Level 10.*

…*Sweet Dreams Inc.* will be the market leader for

"virtual transfers", consisting in the physical termination of human beings and in the migration of their existence onto the corporation's servers, making their customers virtually yours, forever.

31015061R00090

Printed in Poland
by Amazon Fulfillment
Poland Sp. z o.o., Wrocław